Mystery by Moonlight

by MARY C. JANE

Illustrated by RAYMOND ABEL

Cover Design by ETHEL GOLD

SCHOLASTIC BOOK SERVICES

NEW YORK · LONDON · RICHMOND HILL, ONTARIO

To those delightful people, the boys and girls who read my books, and to the understanding teachers and librarians who introduced us to each other.

Contents

A Ghost of a House   5

A Pair of Gold Candlesticks   12

The Small Gray Shed   22

A Stranger in Town   33

A Voice in the Night   42

Tire Tracks in the Grass   51

All the Candy She Could Eat   61

A Clue and a Plan   72

Setting the Trap   83

Only Two Words   91

Locked In   106

Through the Speaking Tube   112

The Secret of Morgan's Green   119

A Ghost of a House

"THIS IS THE BRIGHTEST MOONLIGHT I ever saw," Gail Foster declared, as she and her twin brothers and their friend Conan Prescott started home from the movies.

The boys were arguing about something in the picture they had just seen, and didn't even notice that she had spoken. Gail shrugged her shoulders. Oh, well. It had been foolish of her to go with them tonight, anyway, wasting the last of her week's spending money on a silly picture about a space war. She hurried on up the road so she wouldn't have to listen to their argument.

The moon was almost full on this October Friday night. It turned the empty stretch of road to silver and whitened the roofs of the houses along the way. Gail scuffed the dry leaves and gazed up at the tree branches, black and bare now that the leaves had fallen.

She was far ahead of the boys by the time she approached Morgan's Green and saw its white brick walls gleaming like chalk in the moonlight. The rail fence that surrounded the lawns was chalk-white too, and sparkling with frost.

Gail had never walked past the old house by moonlight before — at least, not all by herself. Even by day it was a strange place, and in the glow of the moon it was ghostly. The black openings that had once been windows and doors looked like real windows and doors again. You couldn't tell that they were only holes in a burned-out shell of a house. You couldn't see the charred beams that had fallen behind the windows, nor the black emptiness within.

Gail's footsteps began to lag a little. She glanced back over her shoulder to see if the boys were coming. They were just rounding a curve in the road and were still a long way behind her.

Morgan's Green was only a ghost of a house. Yet for years — ever since the night it burned — Miss Morgan had sent her hired man to mow the lawns around the ruins and to trim the shrubbery and paint the fence. Nobody else was supposed to set foot on the property. There were "No Trespassing" signs everywhere.

People in the nearby houses hated having the burned-out ruin in their midst. Having the grounds so well kept only seemed to make it worse. It wasn't natural to keep an old ruin standing for years with carefully trimmed lawns and walks and shrubbery around it.

If Miss Morgan had intended to rebuild the place and come back there to live, the neighbors wouldn't have minded so much. But she didn't. She owned a new house at the opposite end of town and was permanently settled there. Yet she kept this old wreck just as it was and wouldn't let anyone go near it.

Gail glanced over the ghostly walls and tall trees to the lights that twinkled along Hillside Road. It was reassuring to see the windows of her own house shining out up there above the shadowed ruins of Morgan's Green.

She brought her slow steps to a standstill and turned to wait for the boys. The night was surprisingly quiet. Not a car passed along Washington Street while she stood beside the fence, waiting. Only the distant rise and fall of the boys' voices broke the silence.

Suddenly a sharp sound of knocking, just behind her, made her whirl around. Someone seemed to be trying to catch her attention, yet there was nothing but the moonlit lawns and the ghostly white walls to be seen. Where could that knocking sound have come from?

In an instant she heard it again, even louder: *rap, rap, rap*.

Her heart hammered. She stared at the empty house. There was nowhere else the sound could have come from.

She shouted to Ted and Tim and Conan, who were already at the corner of the fence. "Come here — quick!"

As they dashed up to her, she held her finger to her lips and whispered, "Listen!"

They stood in a row at the end of the walk, as silent as the very fence posts. But everything was still. Not another sound came from the ruins.

"I heard somebody rap on the walls in there," Gail said. "Honest I did. I heard it twice."

Conan looked around him. "It could have been a tree branch tapping against the wall," he said. "Only it isn't likely, because there isn't any wind."

"I'm sure it wasn't a tree," Gail answered. She rapped on the fence rail with her knuckles. "It sounded like that — only more hollow."

Tim's suggestion that it might have been a woodpecker, Gail dismissed indignantly. "Woodpeckers sleep at night, you nut."

"Gee!" Ted exclaimed. "What if somebody got hurt in there and can't get out? Maybe one of those burned timbers fell on him."

"A person would holler for help, not tap on the wall like a woodpecker," Tim said. He nudged his brother's elbow and added with a nod at Gail, "She's been making up too many stories. Remember the one she wrote about the ghost in the empty schoolhouse? She imagines all that stuff and then she thinks it really happens."

"I do not!" Gail flared. "And you aren't supposed to read my stories. Mamma told you to leave my notebooks alone."

Ted's voice suddenly sounded alarmed. "Hey, maybe it's Katherine who's caught in there!"

He started to run up the walk. Katherine was his dog, a small basset hound, whom he loved and spoiled as if she were a baby. It was a silly name for a dog, but he thought it was the prettiest girl's name he had ever heard.

Tim ran after him and caught him by the tail of his jacket. "Use your head," he muttered. "It isn't Katherine. She couldn't knock on the wall. She'd howl bloody murder if she was caught in there."

Gail and Conan had followed the twins up the walk. They huddled silently together as the light on the walls before them faded all at once to a gray shadow. A small cloud was drifting across the moon. They waited until it passed and the frosty lawns grew bright again. Then Conan, who was the biggest and oldest of the group, resolutely led the way to the house. He peered through one of the window openings.

"Is anyone here?" he called — not very loudly, and with a quaver in his voice.

The twins and Gail looked over his shoulder into the dark interior. Patches of moonlight gleamed upon the fallen beams and heaps of ashes, but nothing stirred or spoke in answer to his call.

"Let's go," Gail whispered nervously, tugging on his arm.

They turned and ran down the walk to the street, not slowing their steps until they were safely around the corner on Hillside Road.

"I have to work at Morgan's Green tomorrow morning helping Hoppy rake leaves," Conan said. "I'll take a good look inside the walls by daylight, if I get a chance. But I don't really believe there is anything there."

The twins made a few more remarks about Gail's funny notions. Then they began to talk about the movie again, as if nothing had happened.

Of course, they hadn't heard the rapping sound, so they had no reason to be frightened. Gail reminded herself of that as she trudged along, hugging her jacket tightly around her. She reminded herself, too, that the boys didn't have any reason to feel guilty about Morgan's Green. They hadn't been trespassing, ignoring the signs on every fence post.

But *she* had.

She thought she had kept it a secret from everyone — the twins, Conan, and even her best friend, Lianne. None of them knew about the small gray shed that was hidden in the tangle of bushes behind the burned house. Gail had only discovered it by accident herself, one day last summer when she was chasing Ted's dog. Katherine had run off with one of Gail's best slippers and seemed to want to bury it in that back yard.

The small toolshed was covered with ivy and hadn't been used for years. When Gail peered through the window and saw the old workbench, with a drawer that would be a perfect place for hiding notebooks and papers, she felt at once that the little, hidden building should belong to her. She had begun that very day to use it as her own private writing room. It was quiet and secret there. She didn't have to worry for fear Ted and Tim would find her stories and laugh at them.

But it *had* been trespassing.

Would she dare to go there any more after this? The sound of the mysterious rapping was loud in her memory. It almost seemed as if somebody knew she had been stealing into the shed behind the old house, and had rapped at her as a warning to stay away.

A Pair of Gold Candlesticks

G<small>AIL AWOKE LATE</small> the next morning. When she saw what a bright, frosty day it was, she leaped out of bed in a hurry. Saturdays were too short, especially at this time of year, to be wasted in sleeping. If she was lucky, she might get a chance to work in her secret writing room today.

"Oh," she whispered, clapping her hand over her mouth, "I forgot. Maybe I shouldn't go there any more."

She began to brush her hair, staring into the mirror without really seeing herself. Usually, things that seemed frightening at night faded into nothing at all by daylight. Yet this morning the memory of the loud rapping on the walls of Morgan's Green was just as disturbing as it had been when it happened.

"This town is getting to be a spooky place," she murmured to her image in the mirror. "Thieves breaking into houses every once in a while, and now — "

She interrupted herself with another startled "O-oh!"

Why hadn't she thought of the robberies last night? The thief who had broken into the other houses in Long Valley might have been looking for something in that old ruin, perhaps in the ell where the rest of Miss Morgan's furniture was stored. If it was he who had made the sounds she'd heard, she didn't need to be afraid to go back to the little gray toolshed. Nobody was after *her*.

She put on her gray corduroy skirt and bright green sweater. Mamma said green was her color, with her dark hair and gray eyes. But as Gail looked at herself in the mirror she wondered if it really made any difference what color she wore. Her hair was short and straight, and her eyes were plain ordinary gray.

"I might just as well wear sky-blue-pink," she muttered, making a face at her own reflection before she turned to go downstairs.

Ted and Tim had already had their breakfast. They were out on the lawn, raking leaves and shouting back and forth to each other, with Katherine barking at their heels.

"Daddy wants you to rake the flower beds, Gail,"

Mrs. Foster said, as she poured cocoa and brought a plate of French toast from the oven. "He says the boys are too rough for that job. Try to get it done before noon, because we're going to Easton to visit Grandpa and Grandma Foster right after lunch."

Gail's eyes grew thoughtful. If the whole family went to Easton, and if they would let her stay home, she would have a good long time to work on her story. She could slip over to her secret place and write for hours. Mr. Hopkins and Conan would be gone by then. Hoppy always went to Miss Morgan's *new* house to work on Saturday afternoons.

Gail finished her breakfast and hurried out to join the twins. To her surprise, she found Ted working all by himself.

"Where's Tim?" she asked, picking up the rake he had dropped on his pile of leaves.

"He went over to Morgan's Green to see if Conan wants to go to Easton with us this afternoon."

"Oh."

Gail raked the peony bed without saying anything more. If Conan went to Grandma's with the others, then nobody would be around to bother her. Still, she was a little bit disappointed. She had meant to ask Conan if he thought the sounds at Morgan's Green last night could have been made by a thief trying to get into the place. He wouldn't think it was just one of her crazy ideas the way the twins would.

Tim returned, a gloomy look on his face. "Conan doesn't want to go," he said.

Ted was surprised. "He doesn't! Why not?"

Tim shrugged his shoulders. "He wouldn't tell me. He didn't want to talk to me at all. I think he's feeling bad about something."

He began to hunt around for his rake. He was too disappointed about Conan to notice that Gail was using it, and went to the garage to get another one.

Gail was worried, too. It wasn't like Conan to refuse to go with his friends. He always loved trips. His own father seldom had time to take his family anywhere. He worked at the woolen mill every day, and his job as county sheriff took every spare minute.

"You don't suppose there's been another robbery, do you?" she asked.

For several months now, Long Valley and the villages on its outskirts had been plagued by one theft after another. A set of old silver, an antique chair, a diamond bracelet, a rare coin collection, and many other valuable things had been stolen. The thief seemed to know when a family was going to be away, or even out for an evening. Although he seldom took more than one or two things from a house, they were sure to be the most valuable things in it. He was so clever he didn't leave a clue of any kind — no fingerprints, no tire tracks, nothing. And nobody ever caught a glimpse of him.

So how could Conan's father, Sheriff Prescott, possibly find out who he was? People in Long Valley were beginning to complain and say that Bill Prescott couldn't handle his job. They talked of choosing a new county sheriff when election time came around.

Mr. Prescott didn't pay any attention to the talk. He went on in his quiet, stubborn way, trying to catch the thief. "I've always got my job at the woolen mill," he would say when his wife or his friends worried about the election in November. "If people think someone else would make a better sheriff than I, let them vote for him. I haven't got time to worry about it."

But Conan didn't feel that way, Gail knew. He was proud that his father was sheriff of the county. Every time a new robbery occurred, it upset him because it made things look worse and worse for Mr. Prescott.

"Conan would have told me about it if there had been another one," Tim said.

Ted leaned on his rake. His round, dark eyes were thoughtful. "Maybe he wouldn't have. He's getting awfully touchy lately. The kids have teased him about the robberies too much."

Gail was thinking so deeply about Conan's father and the thief and — though it didn't seem to have any real connection with them — the strange sounds she had heard last night, she raked too hard and broke the heads off some chrysanthemums. That made her slow down a little. It was noon by the time she and Ted and Tim finished piling the dry leaves and carting them to the middle of the vegetable garden where they could be burned. The twins had to stop and bury each other in the leaves, of course, and then had to pile them all up again before they hurried into the house.

The delicious smell of crabmeat and chili sauce broiled on toast streamed through the door the minute Gail opened it. She sniffed hungrily. It was her favorite lunch. The twins, coming in just behind her, pulled off their jackets and rushed staight to the table.

Daddy had got home from the office and was helping Mamma fix the salad. "Oops, fellers," he said to Ted and Tim. "Those paws of yours don't look exactly lily-white, to me. Hadn't you better run a little water over them?"

The boys giggled and clattered upstairs to get washed.

When they were all seated at the table Gail asked, "Could I stay home this afternoon? I want to finish the story that I'm writing."

"What's it about?" Ted asked, rolling his eyes at Tim and winking.

"I hope it's about Alan Duval again," Tim said. "He bugs me. His black hair and burning eyes and all that stuff."

"And he's so good to his poor old grandmother," Ted added. He and Tim began to giggle until they almost choked on their sandwiches.

Gail's cheeks reddened. "Mamma, you've told them a million times that they aren't supposed to read my stories, and still they do. You and Daddy never do anything about it. Why can't I have a lock on my door, or something?"

Daddy frowned. "There's no need to be so upset, Gail. The boys wouldn't bother to read your stories if you didn't . . ."

"They even read my diary," Gail cried. "They write in it, too, and draw crazy pictures, and tell their friends the things I say."

"They only do it because you get so excited about it," her father tried to explain. "You're just too teasable, Gail. You've got to learn to take a little pestering in your stride."

"It's true the boys ought to leave your things alone," Mamma admitted. "Next time they get into your papers we'll have to punish them. But this —"

Gail didn't listen to anything more. "Next time!"

she thought furiously. "It's always next time. But they never do anything."

"We wouldn't want you to lock yourself in your room," Daddy said. "You stay by yourself too much as it is."

"Like this very afternoon," Mamma added. "Don't you want to see Grandpa and Grandma? They'll be disappointed if you don't come."

The troubled glance that passed between her father and mother was not lost on Gail. She knew she ought to forget about writing her story and say she would go with them as they wanted her to do. But she just couldn't.

Nobody really understood. Mamma and Daddy thought she should be like Ted and Tim, always playing with a crowd of children and never being by herself. They didn't think her stories mattered.

While Mamma was pouring the coffee and serving the apricot sauce and cookies, Daddy said, "Oh, by the way, we've had another robbery in town."

"No!" Mrs. Foster exclaimed, setting the coffee pot down with a thump. "Oh, dear. Won't this ruin Bill Prescott's chances, with election only three weeks away?"

"Where was the robbery?" Tim asked. And his twin demanded, "What was stolen?"

"The thief broke into Mrs. Dryden's house last

night while she was attending the annual meeting of the library board and her son was in New York. He took a pair of gold candlesticks."

Mrs. Foster cried, "Oh, I've seen those candlesticks. They're beautiful. Mrs. Dryden's uncle was ambassador to Spain years ago, and he brought them from there. She was so proud of them!"

"The thief apparently knew their value," Daddy went on. "He didn't take another thing — just the candlesticks."

"I suppose there were no clues this time either," Mamma sighed.

Daddy shook his head. "It's going to make it tough for Bill, all right. A robbery like this right under his nose, and just before election."

"Poor Conan. No wonder he didn't feel like going to Easton with us," Tim said.

"If there were only something we could do!" Mrs. Foster cried. "Some way we could help Bill find out who's committing these crimes!"

"He's clever, whoever he is," Daddy said. "He works fast and never tries to carry off too many things. He must size up the situation ahead of time so he knows exactly when to strike. And what to take."

"It must be someone who knows this town and its outskirts well," Mamma mused. "Why, it may even be someone we know!"

"I'd certainly like to help Bill find out who it is," Daddy said. "And soon, too; otherwise people may be just foolish enough to elect a new sheriff and lose the best man Harwich County ever had on the job. Bill Prescott is a worker — all the Prescotts are."

Gail thought of Conan, working away at Morgan's Green with old Mr. Hopkins every Saturday morning. The Prescotts were workers, just as Daddy said. Yet the thief went right on stealing things without being caught, no matter how hard Mr. Prescott worked at finding him.

She thought of the rapping sounds she had heard last night on the walls of the burned house. At about that time, or a little bit earlier, the thief must have taken the gold candlesticks from Mrs. Dryden's house hardly a mile away.

She started to speak, but hastily closed her mouth and looked down at the table. Nobody else had heard the rapping. If she said anything, it would start more talk from the twins about her queer ideas.

Was it silly to think the thief who stole Mrs. Dryden's candlesticks could have been at Morgan's Green last night? It would certainly have been foolish of him to rap on the walls at her. Yet somebody had done it. The question was: *who?*

The Small Gray Shed

As soon as the rest of the family set out for Easton that afternoon, Gail hurried down Hillside Road and slipped into the tangled yard behind Morgan's Green. A row of spruce trees inside the fence hid her from sight in an instant.

She stole through the orchard to the door of the little toolshed. Blackberry bushes and weeds grew thickly around it. There had once been a path leading to it, but it was choked with underbrush now.

"Nobody has even thought about this shed for years and years," she whispered, with a defiant glance toward the burned house. "Nobody but me."

She lifted the latch and stepped inside. Sunlight was streaming through the one dusty window onto the workbench that she used for her desk. It made the empty little room warm and cheerful.

"It's mine," Gail told herself. "Mine. Ghosts—or thieves — can rap on the walls of the old house all they want to. They aren't going to scare me away."

She pulled out a rain barrel that was tucked under the bench and sat on it. With her elbows on the desk and her chin in her hands, she gazed dreamily through the window. Little tags of leaves were still fluttering on the vines that trailed across the glass.

She tugged at the heavy workbench drawer, pulled out her notebook and pencils, and began to write with excited haste.

> The small gray shed is a secret place.
> Vines climb over it.
> Dry leaves blow in heaps against it,
> And apples bump on the roof and roll to
>   the ground.
> Soon the vines will be bare.
> The leaves will blow away,
> And snow will fall.
> No more red apples,
> No more red leaves.
> The small gray shed will be cold and silent
> All winter long.

She laid down her pencil and lifted her head, her gray eyes aglow. It was fun to write a poem like that, all in a flash. Of course it didn't rhyme. The twins would laugh themselves into a fit if they should read it. But they never would — not if she had to leave it in the workbench drawer all winter.

She read the poem out loud in a low voice, and nodded with satisfaction. It was just the way she felt about this little room. It was easy to write her real thoughts in such a quiet, secret place.

She opened her notebook to her unfinished story, printed "CHAPTER TWELVE" at the top of the page, and began writing again. Except for a few thoughtful pauses to bite her pencil and gaze out the window, she didn't stop until she had raced to the end of the chapter. Then she closed the notebook and began to rub her cold hands together. Her fingers were like ice.

The sun had moved away from the window, and chilly gray light now filled the room. She realized sadly that the days were growing shorter and colder. In another week or two she would have to stop coming here to write. Where could she keep her stories then?

Slowly she tucked her pencils and notebook into the drawer and slid down from the barrel. She was pushing it back into its place under the bench when a quick, sharp knock on the door made her gasp aloud. She turned quickly, her hands pressed against the bench behind her for support.

"It's me, Gail. Don't be scared," a familiar voice called softly. It was Conan!

Before she could answer, he opened the door and slipped inside.

Gail let out a sigh of relief. "How did you know I was here?" she demanded.

"I saw you sneaking in here one day last summer. I've known about you and this toolshed for a long time. When Ted told me you weren't going to your grandmother's this afternoon, I guessed this was where you'd be." He peered curiously around the room. "You can get away from the twins here, huh?"

Gail was surprised at that, and shakily grateful, too. It had been awfully good of Conan to keep her secret all this time. But why did he have to spoil it now by coming here himself? She would never again be able to think of it as her own secret place.

Her gray eyes clouded. "I wish you hadn't come. I wish you hadn't told me you knew about it," she said.

A flush overspread Conan's cheeks. "Heck, I don't care about your secret. I only came to tell you something. I had an idea —" He broke off, his hand on the door latch. "Oh well, skip it."

"No, don't go!" Gail cried, stepping toward him. "I didn't mean to get mad. It's just that I never had any place where I could really be alone until I found this. Tell me what you came to tell me. Please, Conan."

"Well — okay."

She pulled the barrel out again and sat on it while he hitched himself up onto the bench. He clasped one knee with his hands and swung the other foot as he talked.

"Remember last night, after you heard the rapping on the walls and we looked in the window and everything? I said I'd take another look this morning, and I did. I came to work early, before Hoppy got here, and I looked in all the windows. I even went inside."

"Did you discover anything?" she asked.

He shook his head. "There's nothing inside there but heaps of fallen plaster and ashes. There's a big chimney with sooty bricks falling out of it, and there are charred beams lying across everything. But I couldn't find a loose door or board that might have banged in the wind."

"There wasn't any wind last night, anyway," she reminded him. "But if you didn't find out about the rapping, what were you going to tell me?"

He hesitated, swinging his foot more vigorously than before. "I — oh, I don't know. Maybe I shouldn't —"

"Was it about the robbery?" Gail asked. "Was that why you wouldn't go to Easton with the twins?"

Conan stared at her in surprise. "Heck, no, I

wouldn't let that stop me. I know my father will catch the thief one of these days."

As he paused again, Gail demanded, "Well, what in the world is the matter, then?"

"Hoppy fired me," he mumbled, his freckled cheeks flushing a deep red.

Gail stared. She couldn't have been more surprised if he had told her old Mr. Hopkins had taken a whip and beaten him.

"Fired you!" she echoed. "How — how — why would he?"

She went on staring at him while her mind whirled with questions. Mr. Hopkins depended on Conan. And he liked him. He always had, from the time Conan was a little boy in the first grade. He depended on Conan's father, too, to keep mischievous kids and other trespassers away from Morgan's Green. Why, he wouldn't fire Conan. How could he get along without him?

"He's still got those big lawns to rake and all the shrubbery to be trimmed and wrapped up for the winter," Conan went on. "Only last week he said he hoped we'd get time to paint the fence again before it was too cold. He can't do all those things by himself. He's too old."

"Then why? Why did he fire you?" Gail demanded again.

"That's what I'd like to know," he replied. The color faded from his cheeks and his blue eyes flashed. "I always worked hard and tried to do things right. It makes me mad to get fired, as if I hadn't done a good job. Just for no reason."

"Can't you think of anything?" she asked.

He frowned. "I think Hoppy saw me climbing out of the window this morning. He came to work early. I was just climbing over the sill of that back window when he drove into the yard. He didn't say anything then, but maybe he was mad because I went inside that burned part of the house. It was only a little while after that that he told me he wouldn't need me any more this fall."

"But you go in and out of the ell and the garage lots of times when you're working there. You could have looked inside the burned part any day. I don't think Mr. Hopkins would care about that."

"Not unless something — new — was happening around there," Conan said, giving Gail a quick, questioning glance from the corner of his blue eyes.

She was startled. "Something new? Do you mean those rapping sounds I heard last night? Gee, Conan, I've been wondering about them all day."

"There has to be some reason why Hoppy would fire me," he declared. "He needs me, you know. And he used to like me, too."

"I've been thinking about the robberies," Gail said. "Mrs. Dryden's gold candlesticks were stolen at about the same time that I heard the rapping on the walls. Do you suppose the thief could hide things out at Morgan's Green or something?"

Conan thought for a minute, then shook his head. "It wouldn't explain why Hoppy fired me," he said. "*He* wouldn't help the thief or let him hide his stolen goods there. Hoppy's a nice, honest old man. Even if I am mad at him," he added with a sudden grin.

Gail gave a bounce on the hard barrel top. "Maybe Miss Morgan is the one who is helping the thief. She's queer enough. And Hoppy does whatever she tells him."

They fell into a puzzled silence, thinking of Miss Morgan and all that they knew about her. Of course, the queerest thing was the way she held onto the old burned house, refusing to sell it or to let anyone go near it, even though she seemed to have no intention of ever going back to live there herself.

It wasn't as if Morgan's Green had been her old home that she had always lived in and loved. Gail had heard people say that she hardly ever went there to visit her aunt and uncle when they lived in it. And she had only lived in the house a few years, herself, when it burned.

"They say those old folks — Miss Morgan's aunt and uncle — were queerer than she is," Conan mused aloud. "They didn't mingle with people in Long Valley at all. They stayed in that house by themselves all the time, except when friends from the city came to visit them. Hoppy did their errands and looked after them."

"Miss Morgan isn't like that, though," Gail said. "She belongs to everything in town — the church and the clubs and the library board. She's the one who gave that new children's room to the library, and lots of other things."

Conan frowned. "Yeah. And she has plenty of money. She certainly wouldn't bother to steal antique chairs or gold candlesticks."

"No wonder your father is having such a hard time trying to find out who the thief is," Gail sighed. "There just isn't any place to start."

"Well," Conan said, "there is something queer going on at this old house, and I'm going to find out what it is. Even if it doesn't have anything to do with the robberies. I want to know what's wrong with Hoppy and why I lost my job."

He slid down from the bench. "I'm coming back here tonight about nine o'clock. That's the time you heard the rapping sounds. I'll wait around and see if anything else happens."

Remembering the eerie *rap, rap, rap* that she had heard behind those moonlit walls, Gail shivered. "I'll come with you, Conan. It won't be so dangerous if you're not alone."

His blue eyes lighted up. "Gee, that will be great. If we can just get away from the twins! I'm not scared, but it will be more fun with two of us."

A Stranger in Town

Conan opened the door of the toolshed and stepped outside. But before Gail could follow him, he backed into the room again and pushed her back too.

"Somebody's there!" he whispered. "A man. Right behind the house."

He held the door open a crack so they could peek through. A young man in a plaid jacket and corduroy slacks was walking toward the ell, the only part of the house that had not burned in the fire. He carried a notebook under his arm and looked like a college student. Stepping up to the ell window, he tried to peer between the boards that were nailed across it.

"He won't see anything," Conan muttered. "The shades are drawn down tight inside."

The young man wandered around the house, peered into the other windows, tried the door, and even cast a careless glance at the orchard and the shed where the children were hiding. He took the notebook from under his arm and began to write in it.

"It's a sketching pad, I think," Gail whispered. "He must be drawing a picture of the house."

After a few minutes he closed his notebook and sauntered down the driveway. Conan opened the door and took a cautious step along the path. "Wait here, Gail. I want to see where he goes."

She watched Conan dash to the shelter of a tree nearer the house. He waited there, peering around the tree trunk, until he heard the sound of a car starting up. Then he beckoned to Gail.

"His car was in plain sight in front of the house," he said. "He didn't seem to care if anyone saw him. Do you suppose he happened to notice the place and stopped to look it over, just out of curiosity?"

"He must have seen the 'No Trespassing' signs," Gail answered. "Yet he tried the door and looked in all the windows. He even drew a picture of the house."

Conan shrugged. "We'll just have to wait and see if he shows up around here again. We'd both recognize him, that's for sure."

They started back through the orchard to Hillside Road.

34

"Will your folks let you come out tonight as late as nine o'clock?" Conan asked, when they paused outside Gail's house.

She tapped her chin thoughtfully with the knuckles of her left hand. "I could go down to Lianne's house to watch television after supper," she said. "Mamma likes to have me visit her. I'll start for home about nine. Where shall I meet you? In front of Morgan's Green?"

"I'll stop at Lianne's for you," he said.

There was no car in the driveway, so Gail knew her family had not got home. Katherine was yipping wildly just inside the door. It had been a long, lonely afternoon for her.

"Hey, you don't need to knock me down!" Gail exclaimed, as she fumbled for the light over the kitchen table, with the dog nosing at her feet. It was almost dark inside the house. She didn't even take time to hang up her jacket before she started to get Katherine's supper. She opened a can of dog food and was just dishing it out when she heard Daddy's car drive into the yard. Katherine raced to the door, barking more wildly than ever.

After the excitement of the family's arrival had died down a little, Gail helped her mother get supper while Daddy and the boys settled themselves in the living room to wait. The smell of hot rolls and baking beans soon filled the air.

"I'm starved!" Ted cried, coming to the door to sniff and look hopefully around. "Hey, Gail, you should have gone with us. We helped Grandpa make cider with that old hand press he keeps in the cellar. He gave us a jugful to bring home. And Grandma gave us each a new book. I'm starting mine right now."

"She sent something to you, too," Mrs. Foster told Gail. "It's on the hall table."

It was quiet in the lamplit hallway. Grandma's package felt like a book, but when Gail opened it she found a beautiful green diary — a new one for next year. And it had a lock and key!

She clasped it against her chest for a moment, feeling delighted and yet disturbed. She really didn't deserve this nice present, when she hadn't gone to visit Grandma and Grandpa with the others. She bit her lip and whispered, "Next time I *will* go."

But then she remembered what usually happened on her visits to Easton. Aunt Hilda, who lived next door, came over with her two girls. They were almost Gail's age, but not one bit like her. They always ganged up with the twins to play some crazy game. The grownups thought Gail was mean if she didn't join in and have a good time.

She started slowly upstairs with the diary. Just as she reached her own room, the doorbell rang. She heard a man's voice answer her father's greeting. Leaving her diary on her bed, she tiptoed back to the head of the stairs. She glanced down into the lighted hallway and then almost jumped with surprise. The caller was the same young man she and Conan had seen at Morgan's Green.

He was showing his sketchbook to Mr. Foster. "I'm sorry you weren't at home this afternoon," he said. "I sketched your house from what I thought was the best angle, but I'd like you to see it."

Daddy called to Mamma. "Jean, can you come here a minute? It's Steve Craig, the young man who's making our Christmas cards."

Mamma hurried into the hall. "Why Steve, how nice to see you. Is this the picture of our house?"

She and Daddy held the sketch under the lamp, exclaiming delightedly as they studied it. In another minute they were inviting the artist to stay to supper.

Gail watched more and more curiously. This Steve Craig was a handsome young man. She was glad he accepted Mamma's invitation to have supper with them. It would give her a chance to find out what he was really like, and whether he'd had a special reason for prowling around Morgan's Green this afternoon.

From the talk at the supper table she learned that he lived in Harwich, a town about ten miles away. He attended the Greenville School of Design and was earning his way by sketching people's houses for Christmas cards.

"I used to do it summers, when I was in high school," he said, "just in my home town. But now I travel around and do all I can on weekends as well. If I had more time, I think I could develop quite a business."

"It must take up most of your free hours," Mamma said sympathetically. "I hope it doesn't interfere with your schoolwork."

Steve frowned. "I'm painting a series of contemporary landscapes for my special project this term. The Christmas-card business does cut into the time I can give to it, I'm afraid."

Gail broke into the conversation suddenly. "Were you sketching Morgan's Green — that's the burned house on the corner — for your school project?"

The artist looked at her in such astonishment that she hastened to explain, "I was down there this afternoon and I just happened to see you."

"That old ruin interested me," he replied, glancing away from her questioning eyes. "But no, it would hardly do for my landscape series. I'd be more likely to use the rows of cars parked in a factory yard, or a suburban development with houses exactly alike, for that."

He turned to Daddy with a question so far removed from the burned house that Gail couldn't find an excuse to speak of it again. Had he changed the subject on purpose, so she wouldn't ask anything more about it?

As the minutes passed, she found herself beginning to like Steve Craig, in spite of her suspicions. He talked so eagerly about his college doings and his experiences with his Christmas-card business, it was easy to see that he loved it all.

"Do you have a studio of your own to work in?" she asked, when there was a lull in the conversation.

He smiled at her. "I certainly do. At least, I have a room in the attic at home that is all mine. I couldn't do a thing without it." Noticing her wistful expression, he asked, "Why? Do you paint, too?"

She looked down at her plate. "I write stories," she said.

"She thinks nobody should ever read them," Ted told him. "She thinks she needs a studio."

Tim snickered. "You ought to see what she writes. All about this handsome boy with black eyes and broad shoulders . . ."

"That's enough, Tim," Daddy said, while Gail's cheeks flushed crimson.

Steve Craig spoke in a tone more severe than Daddy's had been. "You two boys don't sound very understanding. I can see why your sister would need a place of her own for her writing." He looked the twins up and down and added, "But then, you're rather young. Gail will have to be patient with you."

Ted and Tim drooped like a pair of fat balloons that had suddenly had all the air let out of them. They stared at Steve and then at each other, their round, dark eyes mystified.

Mrs. Foster went to the kitchen to get the apple pie and coffee, and Gail began to clear the table.

"Have you sketched many houses in Long Valley?" Daddy asked their visitor.

"Not many," Steve replied. "I only started here two weekends ago. Let's see — I did the small house across from the school, and Dr. Randlett's farm, and the Dryden house near the library."

The Dryden house!

Gail almost dropped the plates she was carrying when she heard that. This young man seemed as nice as he could be. But he went all over town drawing houses for Christmas cards. He must know a whole lot about the people who lived in those houses. Mrs. Dryden's had been one, and now her gold candlesticks were gone. Steve had been extremely interested in Morgan's Green, too. Walking slowly to her place at the table, she looked again at his candid face and friendly smile. She couldn't forget how he had stood up for her against the twins. She liked him.

"Conan and I had better hurry up and find out what's going on at Morgan's Green," she told herself. "Not just to help Mr. Prescott, either, but for lots of reasons."

A Voice in the Night

MR. AND MRS. FOSTER were glad to have Gail spend the evening with her friend Lianne, as she had known they would be. Everyone liked Lianne, even though she had only lived in Long Valley about a year. Was it because she came from Georgia and talked with a soft southern accent, and called people "honey" all the time? Or because she was so pretty? Gail couldn't decide.

It was almost eight o'clock by the time she set out for her visit. The moon was not very high in the sky. As she turned the corner by Morgan's Green, its silver light was barely visible above the roof. The long shadows cast by the walls covered the lawn and reached clear across the sidewalk. She could hardly keep from running to get out of the ghostly darkness.

"I'd drop dead if I heard the rapping sounds now," she thought.

She scurried across the street to the Welds' front door. Lianne answered her knock, and noticed with surprise how out of breath she was.

"You must be nearly frozen, honey," Lianne said, taking Gail's jacket and kerchief and leading her into the warm living room.

Gail explained that her breathlessness came from being scared, not from the cold. "Morgan's Green was awfully spooky tonight, with the moon just coming up over the roof."

Lianne nodded. "I hate to go past that old house at night. When I take Saucer for his walk at bedtime I usually go toward town, though it's prettier up your way."

Mr. Weld said, "Perhaps you girls won't have to worry about that place much longer. I have a feeling Miss Morgan is fixing to sell it."

"Sell Morgan's Green!" Gail cried, staring at him in amazement. "Why, I thought she never would do that."

"We aren't sure," Mr. Weld said, "but we think it may be so."

"We've noticed Mr. Hopkins moving furniture out of the ell and storing it in the garage," Lianne explained. "That's why we thought Miss Morgan must be planning to sell the old ruin or else have it torn down."

Astonishment slowly gave way to a sharp feeling of disappointment in Gail's heart. If this was so — if Miss Morgan really was going to sell her house — then no wonder Hoppy had told Conan he wouldn't need him any more. He probably felt too upset to want to bother explaining. There wasn't any mystery about it — nothing to do with the robberies, as she and Conan had thought there might be.

And what would happen to the small gray shed in the orchard if Morgan's Green was sold? Gail sighed a long, deep sigh. She would have to give up her secret room for good.

Lianne glanced at her inquiringly. "I didn't think you'd be sorry to have that wreck of a house fixed up," she said.

"Oh, I'm not," Gail replied, with an attempt at a smile. "Not really."

Lianne had a hobby of raising plants, both summer and winter, outdoors and in. She always had some flower coming into bloom that she was sure her friends would want to see. Tonight she took Gail up to her room to admire an Impatience plant with its tiny pink blossoms. They lingered there until Lianne began to shiver.

"Don't you feel cold, honey?" she asked. "Daddy keeps the heat turned low up here. It's fine for my plants, but it's too cold for me. How do y'all stand the winters up here in the North anyway?"

Her voice was filled with wondering admiration, as if she thought it was very brave of Gail to have lived in New England all her life.

They went down to the living room, and with Lianne's father and mother watched a detective story on television. When that was over, the grown-ups left the girls alone to enjoy their favorite program, "The Howland Girls." It was a boarding-school story that the twins and Conan hated, so Gail was surprised to have Conan appear at the door and announce that he thought he'd watch TV with her and Lianne.

She felt a pang of envy. Conan liked Lianne so much he didn't even mind watching "The Howland Girls." Looking at her friend's pale blond hair and the delicate curve of her cheek, lighted up by the glow of the television lamp, she sighed. Some girls were so pretty they were just born to be liked by everyone.

After the program ended, the children visited together for a few minutes until Gail said it was time for her to go home.

Lianne got up. "I'll take Saucer and walk along with you," she said. "It will be nice to have company. That stupid Fred Barney comes along in his car sometimes, and if I'm alone he always wants to give me a ride home. I tell him I'm out for a walk, but he keeps pestering me."

When they were outside, she turned directly to Conan. "Honey, if I was y'all's father, and the sheriff of this county, I know who I'd traipse after if I wanted to catch the thief. Fred Barney, that's who. He knows all the folks around Long Valley. And he doesn't have any regular job. What's he got to do except get into trouble?"

Gail glanced apprehensively at Conan. How would he feel about this suggestion of Lianne's, when he was already so much disturbed about his father's failure to catch the thief?

"Dad has wondered about Fred Barney," he said, after an uncomfortable silence. "He has known him all his life, and he realizes he's kind of a drifter and a spoiled mother's boy. But the Barney family has always been respected around here. Dad can't arrest Fred just because he *might* have done something wrong. He has to have some evidence."

"I wish we could find some, then," Lianne exclaimed.

Gail was surprised at the anger in her voice. It was true that Fred was kind of fresh and silly for a young man in his twenties. He was always going around town trying to sell some useless gadget that nobody wanted. Daddy said the hardest work he did was betting on the horse races at Harwich, and he wasn't much good even at that.

"He *does* go to all the houses in town," she mused aloud. "It gives him a chance to know about people even more than Steve Craig could."

"Who's Steve Craig?" Conan asked at once.

"Oh, I forgot I hadn't told you about him! He's the fellow we saw at Morgan's Green this afternoon." She explained about the drawings he made for Christmas cards, and added, "He sketched Mrs. Dryden's house, too."

Lianne's cocker spaniel tugged on his leash and made the children walk so fast they reached Morgan's Green in hardly a minute. The moon was high above the roof now, and the brick walls gleamed in its light.

"This corner is the spookiest place in Long Valley," Lianne declared. "I'll be right glad to see the old ruin torn down. Our whole neighborhood will be nicer." She put her hand on Gail's arm. "You and Conan wait here until I get back past the fence, will you?"

"We'll walk back with you," Conan said. "There are two of us, and we're not scared."

They didn't speak while they retraced their steps along the sidewalk. The moonlit walls seemed to

cast a spell over them so that they kept their voices low as they exchanged "good-byes" and "see-you-tomorrows" at the edge of the lawn.

Gail and Conan waited until Lianne was back at her doorstep. Then they walked slowly toward their own corner, listening as they went for any sound that might come from the house. Gail, glancing timidly across the silent lawns, felt that she must have imagined anything so impossible as the mysterious rapping she thought she had heard last night.

A few leafless lilac bushes provided a skimpy shelter near the corner. The children sat on the

fence rail there and waited. They were gazing
straight at the house when they heard an unexpected
new sound. Someone was talking inside the walls.
The deep voice seemed to float through the open
front doorway into the moonlit air. Part of a sen-
tence came to them clearly.

"— a few more days, so what's there to —?"

That was all they could catch. The voice trailed
off into an indistinct murmur after that, and then
was gone.

Gail jumped down from the fence. "Somebody's
in there!" she whispered. "Let's go."

But Conan didn't move. The moonlight was

bright enough to show the astonishment on his face. He stared in fascination at the gaping doorway.

She tugged on his arm. "Let's go!" she urged him again.

"We can't go now, just when we might find out something," he said.

Gail cowered behind him, almost too frightened to look at the house. They waited for several long minutes. The moon moved a little higher in the sky, but nothing stirred, and no further sound came from the ghostly ruins.

At last Conan gave up. He left his perch on the fence and started along Hillside Road with Gail, at a run.

Tire Tracks in the Grass

THE TWO didn't stop running until they reached Gail's house. There they paused to catch their breath and to think about what had happened.

"The voice sounded hollow, didn't it?" Gail whispered. "Almost as if it was echoing inside an empty hall. And yet it wasn't very loud."

" '— a few more days, so what's there to —' " Conan repeated. "Was that the way you heard it?"

Gail nodded.

"And then it was just a blub, blub, blub, and silence," he added. "What could it mean? What's there to *what*, for Pete's sake?"

"What's there to worry about?" Gail ventured.

"Hmm. Maybe that was it."

Gail cast a nervous glance down the road. "It's enough to make a person believe in ghosts — those queer taps on the wall last night, and now this."

"Who would hang around inside that ruin, anyway?" Conan asked, frowning. "When I was in there this morning there wasn't a footprint in the ashes, nor anything to show a person had been in there for years."

Gail told him how Hoppy had been moving furniture from the house to the garage. "Lianne's father and mother think Miss Morgan may have decided to sell the place, after all. And if she has, you can see why Hoppy wouldn't need you any more, Conan. He may be so busy getting things fixed up to be sold that he even goes in there at night himself. Maybe it was his voice."

Conan shook his head. "I know the sound of his voice. Besides, he wouldn't walk over here. And there wasn't any car in the yard."

"Well, we can't find out about it, whoever it was," Gail said.

Conan pondered. "Tomorrow's Sunday. If we got up early — about six o'clock — and went back, I could take another look inside the burned walls. Nobody would be around there then."

"I could get my notebooks and pencils out of the toolshed, too," Gail said with a sigh. "If Miss Morgan is going to sell the place, it won't be safe for me to go there any more."

They said good-bye and Gail hurried into the

house. The twins had already gone to bed and she soon went up to her own room. She knew she wouldn't have any trouble waking early. Katherine was used to being let out by six o'clock on weekdays, and on Sundays she whined until Ted got up and opened the door for her.

Gail woke with a start when she heard Ted's slippers flapping on the stairs the next morning. As soon as he was back in bed, she got up and dressed. She buttered a slice of bread, drank some orange juice, then slipped out of the house. Katherine was on the doorstep, yipping joyfully at the idea of having company. There was nothing to do but let her tag along.

Gail glanced up Hillside Road. The sun was just rising, shedding its rosy glow over the trees and houses. Conan wasn't in sight. For a minute she thought of waiting for him right where she was. It would be lonely at Morgan's Green in this early light. But what if he was already there, waiting for her?

With Katherine following at her heels, Gail ran down the hill and slipped under the fence into the grass-grown orchard. Conan didn't seem to be anywhere around. The gray toolshed was silent and empty. When Gail went inside to gather up her notebooks and pencils, she noticed that the red leaves at the window had caught the sunrise light and were as rosy as flowers. This was such a lovely, secret place! Would she ever be able to come back and use it for her story writing again?

As she stepped outside, she began to wonder uneasily about Conan. Where in the world was he? It would soon be broad daylight, with people and cars passing by.

"I wish I dared go into the house by myself," she thought, peering at the shadowed walls.

She stole a few steps closer to the ell. The grass in front of it was stiff with frost. She glanced down at it and was startled to see two dark tracks leading straight across to the doorstep.

She stared at them questioningly. They were tire tracks, no doubt about that. A car must have driven over the stiffened grass during the night.

She was glad to see Conan hurrying toward her from the orchard at that very moment. "My alarm clock didn't work," he explained.

"Look," Gail whispered, pointing to the tracks in the grass.

He whistled softly. "Sa-ay! Someone really has been here."

"In the night, too," she said.

He started toward the house. "I'd better hurry if

I'm going inside. People will be awake in this neighborhood soon."

In the jog where the ell joined the main part of the house, there was one window opening that couldn't be seen from the street. The children crept close to it and Conan scrambled over the sill. Gail watched him pick his way across the heaps of ashes and plaster and charred wood. In some places the floor had caved in and mounds of rubbish filled the cellar hole beneath. The ceilings were wrecked, too. Broken laths and strips of plaster hung down at perilous angles.

When Conan finally returned to the window and climbed out, he was discouraged. "There couldn't have been anyone in there last night," he said. "Heck, it wouldn't have been safe to prowl around that place in the dark."

"It was moonlight," Gail reminded him.

He shook his head protestingly. "It would have been crazy. And yet, the sounds we heard must have come from there. They couldn't have come through the walls from the ell, because the door that used to lead from the ell to the front part of the house has been plastered up."

He shook his head again, as if he just couldn't figure it out.

Katherine began to bark at a squirrel in one of the old apple trees, and Gail ran to pick her up. She and Conan went slowly through the orchard toward home.

"I'd better tell my father about the tire tracks," he said, "and about Hoppy moving furniture to the garage."

"But not about the rapping sound I heard," Gail begged. "He'd think I was crazy."

"I won't tell him about the voice, either. He might think we were both nuts," Conan agreed with a laugh.

He promised to come back later and let Gail know if his father found out anything about the tire tracks.

The rest of that day was a busy time for the Foster family. Mrs. Foster was going to entertain the women's club the next afternoon, so as soon as dinner was over she went to work baking cakes and cookies. Daddy brought some old chairs down from the attic and began to polish and repair them.

"We wouldn't want the ladies to have to sit on the floor," he said, with a wink at Ted and Tim.

The boys were indignant when Mamma handed each of them a dustcloth and sent them upstairs to dust their room. "You wouldn't think it was Sunday," Ted growled.

Gail dusted her room, too. While she was about it she hid her notebooks inside a folded quilt on her closet shelf. The twins might not think to look for them there. She kept watch for Conan, too. The instant she caught sight of him from her window she ran out to meet him, her jacket in her hand. He waited for her at the curve in the road, well away from both their houses.

"Dad went to see Miss Morgan," he said at once, while Gail struggled into her jacket and pushed her flying hair back from her face. "Hoppy was there, too. He said nothing was wrong at Morgan's Green. He was in the ell just this morning, and things were all right. He told Dad that young couples often drive into the yard to park, especially on Saturday nights, and that was probably the reason for the tracks we saw."

"I suppose it could have been that," Gail admitted.

"Dad explained that the neighbors had noticed Mr. Hopkins moving furniture from the ell, and he asked Miss Morgan right out if she was planning to sell the place. And do you know what? She didn't even know Hoppy had moved the stuff!"

"She didn't!" Gail exclaimed. "Then why . . . ?"

"He was worried about the robberies, that's why he did it. Some of the things stored in the ell were valuable, and he was afraid the thief might try to get in there and steal them. He said the garage would be harder to break into."

"Well," Gail said with a sigh, "I guess that explains everything. The tire tracks weren't a clue, after all."

"It doesn't explain why Hoppy fired me, though,"

Conan reminded her. "And it doesn't explain the queer sounds you and I have heard inside the burned walls."

"Was Miss Morgan cross with your father for bothering her about the tire tracks?" Gail asked.

"Gee, no, she was glad he was keeping an eye on things. She even told Dad she was glad Hoppy had me to help him around the place, now that he was getting too old to manage it alone."

"She did!" Gail cried. "What did she say when your father told her Hoppy had fired you?"

He hesitated. "He didn't tell her."

"Well, for goodness' sake, why not?"

"He didn't know about it. I haven't told him yet."

Gail couldn't think of anything to say. She understood, all of a sudden, how awfully bad Conan felt about losing that job. And she didn't blame him.

"I'm getting sick of that old Morgan's Green," she muttered. "I wish we'd never heard of the place."

He grinned. "Now don't get mad, Gail. Something good came of those tire tracks and Dad's visit to Miss Morgan, just the same."

She gave him a doubting glance and only sniffed in answer.

"Yes it did," he insisted. "Miss Morgan is so worried for fear my father may not get re-elected next month that she wants to do something to help him. She is going to offer a reward — a hundred dollars' reward — to anyone who gives him information that leads to the thief's arrest."

"A hundred dollars' reward!" Gail exclaimed. "Gee, everybody will be looking for clues."

"But we are the only ones who will be looking for them at Morgan's Green," he said. His voice and his deep blue eyes were sober. "That's the place to look, Gail, no matter what you say. And we're the only ones who know it."

All the Candy She Could Eat

O<small>N</small> M<small>ONDAY</small> <small>AFTERNOON</small> when Gail, Ted, and Tim got home from school, they found the driveway and the road in front of the house lined with cars. The house was full of ladies who were talking and having tea. The boys wouldn't even go in. They dashed off up the road to play with Conan.

Gail stole into the kitchen. The table was loaded with plates of cookies, sandwiches, and cakes. One of the ladies who was helping Mamma serve tea told Gail to take anything she wanted.

"Your mother always has more than we can possibly eat," she assured her, smiling.

Gail stood in a shadowed corner while she drank a glass of milk, munched some cookies, and listened to the chatter in the living room. Miss Morgan was there, and the ladies were asking her all kinds of questions about the big reward she had offered.

"Just for information?" one woman asked, as if she couldn't believe it. "Do you mean that if we caught sight of the thief's car and gave Bill Prescott the license number, we might get the reward?"

"That's it, exactly," another voice exclaimed. "We don't have to catch the thief ourselves. Just find a clue."

Gail frowned as she listened. Everybody in town was going to start hunting for clues. What chance would she and Conan have to do something the grownups couldn't do?

Supper was fun that night, after the ladies had gone. The family always had frozen TV dinners on club-meeting nights, and the children loved them even if Daddy didn't. For dessert there were the left-over cakes and cookies — you could eat dozens of them if you wanted to.

"And candy," Ted sighed blissfully, gazing at the dishes of chocolate-covered mints and nuts that had hardly been touched.

Mamma was too weary to notice how much Ted and Tim ate that evening. As soon as the rooms were picked up and the supper cleared away, she and Daddy slumped down on the living-room couch to listen to records on the hi-fi.

Gail knew the twins would hang around downstairs as long as the candy lasted. It would be a good time for her to go to her room and write. She wanted to set down everything that had happened at Morgan's Green since she had heard the strange rapping sounds on Friday night. It might help her and Conan figure things out.

She worked at it for almost an hour. When she finished, she put the notebook back inside the folded quilt and went downstairs. Ted and Tim were playing checkers at the kitchen table, and Katherine was sitting in Ted's lap. Her ears drooped and her eyes looked more mournful than usual.

Gail got an apple from the refrigerator. "I couldn't eat another piece of candy if you paid me," she said. "I'm sick of it."

"Katherine isn't," Ted said, taking a half-melted chocolate mint from his pocket and poking it into the dog's mouth.

Gail looked again at the drooping animal. "I think she's had too much of that stuff."

Tim jumped two of his brother's kings and then peered at Katherine himself "Yeah, Ted, you'd better lay off. She's had enough."

"She loves it," Ted declared. "This may be the only time in her life that she will be able to have all the candy she can eat." Defiantly, he put another chocolate in her mouth. "I want to see how much candy a dog will eat when she has a chance. Do you know how many chocolates Katherine has had already?"

His brother and sister stared at him. "You mean you've been counting them?" Gail cried. And Tim demanded, "How many?"

"Twenty-one," Ted replied in a satisfied tone. "How's that for a record? I bet she'll eat thirty before she stops. I bet there isn't another dog in town that —"

Katherine suddenly scrambled down from his lap. She trotted to the door and stood there with her head hanging. She didn't even whine to go out.

Gail hurried to open the door for her. "Poor little thing," she murmured, as Katherine waddled slowly out onto the step.

Ted wasn't disturbed. "She's all right. She always likes to go out before she settles down for the night."

"I'm going for a little walk in a minute," Gail said. "Maybe I'll take her with me."

She continued to watch the checker game until the hands of the kitchen clock moved close to nine. Then she went to the door to see if Katherine was still there. The step was empty. She whistled and called, but the dog didn't come.

"I'll get her. She'll come for me." Ted declared. Leaving the kitchen door wide open behind him, he whistled his loud, piercing whistle, over and over, and very much off key. He kept it up until Daddy shouted from the living room, "For Pete's sake, shut that door!"

Ted came in, banging the door behind him. His dark eyes were worried. "This is the first time she ever refused to come when I whistled for her at bedtime. Something must have happened."

"Something happened, all right," Tim said grimly. "You gave her too many chocolates, that's what happened."

"She looked sick when she went out," Gail added.

"We'd better go look for her," Ted muttered.

He and Tim grabbed their jackets and Gail hurried to get hers. She couldn't help worrying about the little dog.

The full moon was high in the eastern sky. Its strange, colorless light flooded the fields and pastures along the road.

"It should be easy to find her," Tim said. "We can see everything as plain as day."

They went to the foot of the hill, listening as they went for Katherine's bark, and searching the edges of the road for her huddled form. At the corner, by the white rail fence of Morgan's Green, they paused to look down Washington Street.

"She never comes down here," Ted said. "She's afraid of the traffic."

While they hesitated, wondering what to do next, Gail looked across the lawns at the walls of the old house. She listened intently for the sound of a voice or a tapping. But the silence was unbroken until Ted began to whistle for Katherine again.

"Maybe she went in the other direction, toward the Prescotts'," Tim suggested. "We'd better go back."

When they were halfway up the hill, they saw Conan coming along. The twins hailed him eagerly. "Where are you going? Have you seen Katherine anywhere?"

"I'm just taking a walk," he answered. "I stopped at your house, but you were gone. Can't you find your dog?"

"Ted fed her twenty-one chocolates," Tim told him disgustedly. "We think she's gone off by herself because she's sick."

"Whew!" Conan whistled. "Twenty-one chocolates would be enough to give a horse a stomachache."

"Let's go look in the pasture behind our house," Ted urged, his voice beginning to sound alarmed. He set off up the hill at a run.

"You go with him, Tim," Conan suggested. "Gail and I will look around down this way some more."

When the twins were out of earshot, Gail said in a low voice, "I listened at the fence corner a few minutes ago. There's nobody at Morgan's Green tonight. It's awfully quiet, and the moon is so bright you can see everything."

"But we have to keep listening there every chance we get," Conan replied. "We can't tell when those queer sounds might come again."

They were standing in the middle of the road, not far from the row of spruces that hid the ruins, the orchard, and the small gray shed from sight. Gail tried to peer under the branches.

"Katherine likes to hide bones in that back yard. That's how I discovered the toolshed. I was chasing her one day because she was running off with one of my slippers. I think she was going to bury it in there, the way she used to do with her bones. It's a good place to get away from people. Do you suppose she could be in there now?"

The yard behind Morgan's Green was a good place to hide from people, all right. The darkness under the spruce trees was as black as ink. Beyond them the orchard was a weird patchwork of silver light and twisted shadows.

"I don't know as I dare go in there," Gail whispered.

But Conan was determined. "We could go as far as the shed. You could call to Katherine and we could wait for her a while."

He vaulted over the fence and held back the branches of a spruce tree so Gail could get past. They tried to keep in the shadows all the way across the orchard. As they drew close to the shed, they heard a feeble whimper. Katherine was lying on a heap of drifted leaves near the shingled wall.

Gail picked her up. Her nose was hot and her head drooped limply.

"Poor little pet," Gail whispered, stroking her soft fur.

"Let's wait a few minutes before we take her home," Conan urged. "She's only got a stomach-ache. She'll be all right."

They leaned against the shed door and gazed toward the house. The ell and the back doorstep were in deep shadow. Katherine began to tremble as if the silence and darkness frightened even her. Gail rubbed her soft ears and started to croon a comforting word, when Conan whispered sharply, "Listen!"

A distant sound, like the voice of someone passing along Washington Street, was all she heard at first. As the sound deepened and grew louder, she realized that it was coming from the burned part of Morgan's Green, like the voice they had heard on Saturday night. This time none of the words could be understood.

"Wait here," Conan whispered.

He darted away before she could try to stop him, and was soon lost in the shadows nearer the house.

Gail shrank back against the toolshed wall, hugging Katherine against her like a shield. The moonlight was full upon her face. What if somebody looked this way and saw her? She felt the latch of the door digging into her back and thought wildly of slipping inside for safety, but she was too frightened to stir from where she was.

Katherine lifted her head to stare in the direction of the house. She growled low in her throat.

Gail wondered if her sensitive ears caught sounds that humans couldn't hear.

She cuddled the dog gently, murmuring, "It's all right. Don't bark now, whatever you do."

A minute later, when Conan stepped out of the shadows almost at her elbow, she gave a stifled shriek. "Ooh, you scared me! I didn't hear you coming."

"We'd better go," he said, taking hold of her arm.

70

"Did you see anyone?"

He shook his head. "I heard two men talking, but I couldn't tell a word they said."

He hurried her along, keeping in the shadows of the orchard trees as much as possible.

"I think Katherine heard the voices," Gail said. "She growled and looked toward the house."

"But where could anyone have been?" Conan asked. "There's nothing inside those walls but ashes and bricks and boards. I even looked in the cellar and up the chimney, the other morning. There is hardly a spot that isn't heaped with rubbish. Nobody would hang around in there."

As they stepped out onto Hillside Road, he added slowly, "One of the voices sounded familiar to me. I know I've heard it before, but I can't remember when or where."

Ted and Tim came racing down the hill toward them at that minute. They were so glad to see Katherine they couldn't talk of anything else. Morgan's Green and its ghostly voices would have to be forgotten until tomorrow.

A Clue and a Plan

CONAN AND THE TWINS stayed at school for a Scout meeting on Tuesday afternoon, so Gail and Lianne walked home together.

"Everybody is talking about that reward Miss Morgan is going to give," Lianne said. "Some of the kids are trying to get it. I'd be scared to try to catch a thief, myself."

"You don't have to catch him to win the reward," Gail reminded her. "You just have to find some clues that will help Sheriff Prescott catch him."

"Well, honey, I don't aim to get mixed up in it," Lianne said, with a toss of her blond head.

"You've got a suspect," Gail teased her. "You said Fred Barney was the one you would go after, if you were sheriff."

Lianne caught Gail's arm. "Why did you even mention him? 'Speak of the devil and he's sure to appear.' There's his car in front of my house right now." She stamped her foot. "Let's not go in."

But Gail had a sudden idea. "I want to ask him something. I think I can find out where he was Friday night. Let's stop for just a minute."

Fred was in the living room, talking to Mrs. Weld about a new kind of can opener he was selling. He smiled at Lianne and asked, "How's the sweet honey child this afternoon?"

She didn't answer. She and Gail perched on the sofa across the room from him. When Mrs. Weld went out to the hall to get her purse, Gail spoke hesitatingly about the space picture she had seen at the movies on Friday night. "Did you like it?" she asked Fred.

He looked confused. "Like it? I didn't see it."

"I thought you were there," she insisted.

He laughed scornfully. "Me, at the movies on a Friday night when all the kids in town are there? I should say not. I was in Harwich Friday night." He turned to Lianne's mother, who had returned with the money. "I drove my mother and some friends to that same bridge party you went to."

Mrs. Weld smiled. "I guess you and the other men had a pretty good time with that game of your own, while you waited."

Lianne started toward the door. "I'm going to Gail's house, Mamma," she said.

She and Gail hurried out, ignoring Fred's "So long, honey child."

Gail sighed. "Well, we'll have to cross him off the list. He couldn't have stolen Mrs. Dryden's candlesticks last Friday night. Or rapped on the walls."

Lianne stared. "Rapped on what walls?"

"Oh dear, I wasn't going to tell you about that," Gail said.

Falteringly, she began to explain about the

sounds she had heard on her way home from the movies that night. They were passing Morgan's Green at the moment, and Lianne stared at the ruined house. It looked peaceful in the golden afternoon light, but her eyes were frightened. "I bet it *is* haunted," she whispered. "I think something bad must have happened there. Maybe somebody murdered that queer old aunt and uncle of Miss Morgan's. Maybe that's why spirits rap on the walls on moonlit nights."

Gail cried incredulously, "Lianne! You don't really believe anything so crazy as that."

Lianne's wide forget-me-not blue eyes were clouded. She nodded vigorously. "I sure do believe it. I'm not going to walk past here after dark any more. I don't believe in troubling the spirits."

Gail didn't know what to say. She had been frightened by the eeriness of Morgan's Green at night herself. But it wasn't spirits or ghosts she was afraid of. Not really.

She was glad to get home and forget about ghosts and robberies for a while. There were still lots of cookies left from Mamma's club meeting, and she made some hot cocoa to go with them.

"Let's take our cups out on the back steps," she suggested to Lianne. "It's nice and sunny there."

When they were settled, Lianne glanced up the

road toward Conan's house. "Did you know that some people think Sheriff Prescott may be helping the thief get away with the antiques and things that have been stolen?" she asked.

"No!" Gail stared at her friend in horrified amazement. "What an awful thing to say! How could anyone believe it?"

"Don't quarrel with *me*, honey," Lianne protested. "*I* don't believe it. But my daddy says lots of folks do. They think it's queer that Mr. Prescott never finds any clues. They say he ought to be able to track down some of the stolen goods, if he was really trying So they think maybe he doesn't want to catch the thief."

Gail bit her lip. "He is trying. I know he is."

"It scares me to think about those robberies," Lianne confessed. "Sometimes I hardly dare to go to bed at night, for fear the thief might get into our house. And now that you've told me about the rappings at Morgan's Green —" She broke off, shivering as if she had really seen one of the "spirits" she talked about.

"Let's go look at Mamma's chrysanthemums," Gail suggested, putting her arm around Lianne's waist. She felt sorry for her. It was too bad to be scared of things like ghosts that weren't even real and couldn't hurt you.

There were still a few shaggy white blossoms on the chrysanthemum stalks, though the gray-green leaves were beginning to curl and turn brown. In her pleasure in sniffing the flowers and examining the soil around them, and asking questions about what Mrs Foster did to keep plants from being winter-killed in this cold northern region, Lianne forgot her fright. When she went home, Gail walked all the way past Morgan's Green with her.

When Gail returned and went into the hall to hang up her jacket, her mother called to her from the kitchen. "Gail, will you straighten out the coats and hats and rubbers in that closet? I pushed everything back to make room for the ladies' things yesterday."

Gail had already noticed how bare the hooks were. She turned the light on and began to move the coats from the back of the closet. With her arms heaped high, she suddenly stumbled over something soft and flexible under her feet.

"Oh, Katherine!" she exclaimed. "Excuse me."

Then she looked down over her mound of coats and began to laugh. What she had stumbled over was one of Daddy's old overshoes, and not Ted's little dog.

She hung the coats on their hooks and stooped to

pick up the overshoe. Crumpled under it was a sheet of letter paper. She glanced at it casually, and then her eyes narrowed into a puzzled frown.

. . . burned several years ago, I believe. The ruins of the house are on the main street of the village and are set among wide, well-cared-for lawns. I understand the present owner lives in the town somewhere. Hope you find what you are looking for, Steve.

We miss your weekend visits. If the tuition keeps going up at the School of Design, you'll have a —

Gail read the sentences several times. Then she folded the paper and tucked it into her blouse pocket. Slowly, thoughtfully, she went on with her job of bringing order to the jumbled closet.

Her thoughts were an even wilder jumble. Steve Craig must have lost that letter. It must have dropped out of his pocket when Daddy hung his coat here on Saturday night. What had the person who wrote it meant when he said, 'Hope you find what you are looking for, Steve'? She remembered how the young man had peered into the windows of Morgan's Green and tried the door of the ell.

Steve Craig was an artist. He probably knew all about antiques and beautiful old things like those that had been stolen in Long Valley. He had sketched Mrs. Dryden's house and could have known about her candlesticks —

She closed the closet door and leaned against it with a sigh. If only she hadn't liked Steve so much! If only she could keep from remembering how he had put the twins in their place when they had teased her. He understood about her stories, and how she needed a place of her own for writing them. She didn't want him to be the thief.

Gail could hear the twins, just home from their Scout meeting, telling Mamma about it. Under cover of their conversation, she snatched up her jacket and ran out to see if she could catch up with Conan. She wanted to show him the letter.

It was almost dark outside. She flew up the road and overtook him at the curve that hid his house from sight. It was too dark for him to read the letter, but she told him all about it.

"Steve Craig can't be the thief. He's too nice," she declared.

"But what could he be looking for at Morgan's Green?" Conan asked.

What indeed? Try as she would, Gail couldn't think of any good, honest reason why he should have been hunting around there.

"I *wish* we could find out what's wrong with that darned old place," she muttered.

"I've thought of a way we might find out," Conan told her.

Gail hugged her jacket around her with an excited shiver. "What is it?"

"You know that portable tape recorder Lianne got for Christmas? If she would lend it to us, we could set it inside the burned walls some night. The next day we could play the tape back and hear what was said. Maybe we could even tell who was doing the talking."

Gail felt disappointed. One objection after another leaped into her mind. "The tapes on the recorder only run for about half an hour. How could we be sure someone would talk in there just after we put the recorder inside the door? And how could we turn it off when the tape had run through?"

"We couldn't. But it wouldn't matter. The batteries would run out after a while, and the recorder would stop by itself. We could put in new batteries the next day — they don't cost much. And we'd have to keep trying it every night until we did catch the voices."

Gail was silent. She was thinking of Lianne's fear

of "spirits" and of Morgan's Green. She wouldn't like Conan's idea.

"We'd better not tell Lianne what we want to do with the recorder," she said finally. "I don't think she'd like it. We could just borrow it for a while."

Conan's voice was indignant. "Lianne is a good sport. She'll be glad to help us. We should have told her about our plans long ago. She lives so near to Morgan's Green, she could keep watch on the place for us. She's always glad to help anyone. You know that."

"Well, we can ask her," Gail said.

She didn't tell him what Lianne had said about the old ruin and how frightened she was of it. Maybe she would be feeling differently by to-morrow. Anyway, if she really did believe in spirits and haunted houses, she could explain to Conan herself. Gail wasn't going to tell.

Setting the Trap

CONAN WAS WAITING for Gail when she came out of the school building the next afternoon. "Where's Lianne?" he demanded at once.

"Oh, she stayed to help Miss Allen arrange some new plants in the window boxes in our room," Gail explained. "She won't be long."

He glanced across the playground. Ted and Tim were standing near the maple tree, arguing about whether or not they should go over to the high school to watch football practice.

"We'd better start home before they decide to come with us," he said. "We can wait for Lianne at her house. I want to ask her about that tape recorder."

Nobody answered their knock when they reached the Welds' front door. They sat down on the step to wait. They soon saw Lianne approaching. Sally

Wilson was with her, and Ted was tagging along behind them, looking lost without his twin.

"We don't want him to see us," Gail cried.

She and Conan crept across the porch to a spot where a fir tree near the railing hid them from sight. They watched the others lag along toward them, and Gail's gray eyes darkened with indignation when she saw Ted sneak up behind Lianne and snatch her new blue beret from her blond head. He flung it into the leaf-filled gutter, and then drew back to see what she would do.

Lianne picked up her cap and put it on, talking and laughing with Sally all the while. She didn't even notice Ted.

"She should have slapped him," Gail whispered. "Now he'll do it again."

This time Ted tossed the blue cap into the middle of the street. It was just luck that a car didn't come along and run over it. But Lianne kept on with her conversation while she went after it, and still didn't say a word to Ted. Was she going to let the pest get away with his tricks?

Even Conan was indignant when Ted stole the beret for a third time. "Brother! He sure is asking for trouble," he muttered.

Lianne rescued her cap once more and patted

it onto her hair. She walked serenely on until she and Sally were in front of her house. There, Ted made a last hasty grab at the beret and hurled it across the lawn.

Lianne turned to face him, and Gail whispered gleefully to Conan, "Now he'll get it!"

Lianne's blue eyes were full of bewilderment. She stared at Ted for a few seconds, shaking her head as if she couldn't understand him. He stared back at her warily, poised for instant flight.

Finally, in her gentle drawl, she asked, "What in the world are y'all trying to do, honey?"

Surprise and embarrassment chased the mischief from Ted's dark eyes. He picked up her cap, gave it a quick dust-off, and handed it to her politely. Then he darted across the street without answering her question.

Gail's face was as bewildered as Lianne's had been. Was this the reason people liked southern girls so much? Not because they were pretty and had a soft drawl and called everyone honey, but just because they were nice? Just plain nice?

She thought of the way she would have acted if anyone had pestered her like that. When the twins teased her, she cried and stormed around until she made the whole family miserable. She sighed.

How did people learn to be good-natured about things — not just once in a while, but all the time?

Conan stood up and called a cheerful "Hi!"

"Lawsy, you scared me!" Lianne exclaimed, clasping her hands to her chest. "What are you doing, hiding like that?"

Gail scrambled to her feet. "We wanted to ask you about something, and we didn't want Ted to know."

They sat down on the steps while Conan began to explain about his father's problems, and his lost job with Hoppy, and the voices he and Gail had heard at Morgan's Green.

"Voices?" Lianne asked, with a questioning glance at Gail. "I thought you said you heard a rapping sound on those old walls, honey?"

Gail nodded. "I did. But the next night we heard voices in there, too."

Conan told of the tire tracks in the grass and the letter Gail had found in the closet. "We think there must be some connection between Morgan's Green and the robberies here in town," he said.

"And if we could borrow your tape recorder and put it inside the ruins tonight, we might find out who the men are and what they are doing in there," Gail added.

"You come with us," Conan suggested. "It will be safer with three of us. If we find a clue to the thief, we'll all share the reward."

Lianne shook her head violently. "I wouldn't go near that old ruin, not even if there was a bushel of diamonds hidden in there. And you shouldn't, either. It's dangerous." She shivered. "The only thing to do with spirits is to leave them alone."

Conan was puzzled. "Spirits? Do you mean ghosts? Heck, there aren't any ghosts at Morgan's Green. That voice we heard was real. Even Gail's dog could tell that. We want to find out who it is."

Lianne was stubborn. "Honey, you don't know about spirits. There was an old man down where I came from who was queer in his head all his life. He got that way from going into a haunted house when he was just a little boy. On a moonlight night, too. Everybody who knew him said he was a smart young one until he did that." She clasped her hands together pleadingly. "Don't go back to that old house. Please don't!"

Conan stared at her as if he had never seen her before. "But there aren't any spirits there. Morgan's Green isn't haunted."

Gail put her arm around Lianne. "We know the voice was real. If you'll just let us borrow the tape recorder, we may find out who it was. It might help Conan's father, you know. Will you let us have it, Lianne?"

"I don't care about the tape recorder," she mumbled. "Y'all can take it if you want to."

"We may not have to go inside the place," Gail reassured her. "Conan can just set it in the doorway."

On the way home, Conan asked, "Will you be able to go with me tonight? We ought to wait until nine o'clock or so, because the tape is only good for half an hour."

"I think so. I'll take a little walk, if Mamma will let me. I'll start at nine sharp."

Gail had forgotten that it was Wednesday. Her father and mother always visited their friends the Bakers on Wednesday evenings. And the twins had favorite television programs then, too. It was going to be easy to meet Conan.

The moon was low on the horizon when she stepped out of the house at nine o'clock. She almost bumped into him in the darkness.

"Let's hurry," he said. "It should be easy to sneak into the old place if the light stays as dim as this."

"You won't go inside, will you? It's so dark you might fall into the cellar."

Conan's voice was confident. "I'll just set the recorder going and put it inside the door. It won't take a minute."

As they started across the shadowed lawn, Gail whispered, "Nobody could see us, that's for sure."

She stayed close behind him while he picked his way toward the doorstep. She couldn't even make out where the windows and doors were in the blackness that loomed before them.

Conan stopped suddenly. A faint sound, as of something being dragged across a floor, seemed to come from the empty ruin. It lasted only a second or two, so that Gail could hardly be sure she had heard it. Neither she nor Conan said a word. The silence deepened around them while they hesitated in the frosty grass. Moonlight brightened the corners of the house and gleamed through one of the windows, shedding a path of light across the vacant space inside.

Conan took a quick step forward. He reached the stone doorstep and bent down to find a place for the recorder. As he did so, the dragging sound began again, continued for a second or two, and stopped.

Gail shrieked, and Conan raced down the walk, pausing only to grasp her hand and pull her along with him. They didn't stop running until they were halfway up Hillside Road.

"I dropped the recorder," he gasped, when he had caught his breath.

"You couldn't have dropped it far," she said. "It'll be all right."

He stood still for a minute. Then he said in a troubled tone of voice, "That old ruin was empty, wasn't it? You could just feel how empty it was."

He gazed into her face as if he wanted her to assure him that someone really had been there, making that mysterious sound. They both turned to look back, but Morgan's Green was out of sight behind the sharp black spires of the spruce trees. Without a word, they began to run toward home, as fast as if all of Lianne's "spirits" were chasing them.

Only Two Words

A LIGHT RAIN was beginning to patter on the dry leaves when Gail hurried out of school the next afternoon. She saw Conan dashing up Washington Street, and she dashed after him. When he came out of Morgan's Green with the tape recorder in his hands, she was at the fence to meet him.

"I think it worked all right, even if I did drop it," he told her. "The tape unwound onto the other spindle, the way it was supposed to do."

They ran all the way to his house, in their eagerness to get there without having the twins at their heels. Conan rushed right to the sun porch that was his favorite retreat.

"It will take a few minutes to rewind the tape and put in the new batteries," he said, closing the glass doors to the living room behind him.

When all was ready, they bent their heads over the machine to listen. At first there was only the

steady whir of the unwinding tape, although Gail almost thought, now and then, that she heard the same faint dragging sound she had heard last night, above the whir.

Ten minutes went by without anything but the sound of the machine. Conan stirred restlessly, and Gail asked, "Do you suppose that's all?"

He put his finger across his lips and bent his head even closer to the recorder. A crackling sound came from it, and an undercurrent of voices. The two children looked at each other with excited eyes. This was what they had been hoping for!

After a few minutes their excitement began to ebb. There certainly were voices, but they were too low and indistinct to be understood.

"I can't make out a word," Gail declared.

And then, suddenly, a single phrase did stand out clearly from the murmur of sounds.

"*At Fowler's —*"

Gail looked inquiringly at Conan. He shook his head. "I never heard of anyone by that name around here."

They waited anxiously for the last of the tape to unwind. When it stopped Conan groaned, "Oh, *great!* Two words that don't mean a thing — that's all we get for our trouble."

"It proves somebody really was inside that empty old house," Gail said. "Wouldn't your father believe it if we played this tape for him? Wouldn't he do something?"

He shook his head. "It doesn't prove anybody was in there who had no right to be. I suppose it could even have been Hoppy and some friend of his, though it didn't sound like him. Dad won't want to bother Miss Morgan again unless he's sure there is something wrong."

The memory of what Lianne had told her about Mr. Prescott stirred unhappily in Gail's mind. Was he really trying to catch the thief? If he was, he ought to be eager to follow every least little clue.

She noticed, all at once, how dark it had grown outside the sun-porch windows. "I'd better go home. It's getting late."

"This tape-recorder idea of mine was a real flop," Conan sighed in discouragement.

"You said we might have to try putting it inside Morgan's Green more than once," she reminded him.

He squared his shoulders. "Yeah, that's so." Glancing at the raindrops on the windows, he added, "Not tonight, though. The rain might spoil Lianne's recorder. We'll have to wait until tomorrow. We could try a different time. Before supper, maybe."

Gail agreed to that and hurried home, feeling more discouraged than she had admitted. Lianne's recorder didn't seem to be powerful enough to pick up words and repeat them clearly. Was it any use to try again?

It was still damp and gray and cold when they came out of school the next afternoon. They had no chance to make plans, because Lianne and the twins were right beside them.

"Let's have a game of checkers up at our house," Ted proposed. "It's Friday, so we ought to do something special."

"I have my music lesson at four thirty," Lianne said. "But I'll come up for an hour or so."

A holiday mood overtook them all when they settled down in the living room with their game. Mamma had a fire burning in the fireplace, and she let Ted pour some of Grandpa Foster's cider for everyone. Gail was glad to postpone any thought of going back to Morgan's Green. It was easy to forget the cold and fogginess outdoors as the fire snapped out little showers of orange sparks and the game grew more and more lively.

At quarter past four by the mantel clock, Lianne jumped up. "I've got to go, or I'll be late for my lesson."

Ted hurried to the closet to get her jacket, something Gail had never known him to do for anyone before. He got her blue beret, too, and gave it a quick brushing before he handed it to her, as if he were worried that there might be the least speck of dirt on it. A fine time to think of that, after the way he had thrown it around only a day or two ago!

He called to Tim, "Hey, let's go downtown and see if the new *Space Era* magazine has come in, huh? We can walk back with Lianne."

Tim agreed, and the three of them set out together, while Gail and Conan picked up the cards and cider glasses.

"I'll go home and get the tape recorder," he whispered. "We'll just about have time to take it to Morgan's Green before supper."

Gail went with him almost reluctantly. It was a discouraging afternoon, with the cold mist in the air and darkness creeping on. As they approached the old house, she said, "I'm going inside too. I want to see what it's really like in there."

They slipped through the doorway into the blackened interior. Conan edged warily around the heaps of rubbish to the big chimney in the center of the house.

"Did you ever look up the flue?" Gail whispered.

"Of course. That was one of the first things I thought of. There's nothing there. You can see right up to the sky."

He moved around the chimney toward the wall of the ell. Gail followed uncertainly, peering into the dim corners of the room as she went.

Rap, rap, rap!

She shrieked as the hollow knocking sounded from the walls behind her. Then she clasped her hands over her mouth and stared around the empty room.

Conan ran to the back window. "Let's get out of here!"

He stopped suddenly, and Gail bumped into his shoulder as she plunged after him.

"What's the matter?" she gasped.

"The ell door is open," he whispered. "Somebody must be in there."

For a few seconds, in which it seemed to Gail that the beating of her heart was louder than the ghostly rapping had been, they stood motionless with their backs pressed against the wall. Then she began to run, leaping over the piles of rubbish as if they were no more than tufts of grass. She was out the front door before Conan could catch up with her.

"We ought to wait," he puffed, as they fled down the walk. "We ought to find out who it is."

Gail's only wish was to get across the bare, open stretch of lawn to the safety of the sidewalk. Once they were there, nobody could be sure they had been inside the old ruin at all.

They had almost reached the corner of their own road when they heard footsteps pounding out the driveway of Morgan's Green. At the same moment the streetlight over their heads came on, trapping them in its circle of brightness.

A voice called, "Hey, kids, wait a minute!"

Gail recognized the voice, and her heart sank. It was Steve Craig.

He came running up to them. "Say, were you inside that old house just now? Was it you who rapped on the wall at me?"

Gail stared. "We didn't rap . . ." she started to explain.

But Conan interrupted her. "We were just poking around in there," he said. "What were you doing?"

Steve let out a breath of relief. "Thank goodness it was only you! That rapping scared me half out of my wits." He paused to draw another long breath, while the children watched him with puzzled, half-frightened eyes. If Steve didn't do that rapping, who did? *Who* did?

Steve looked up into the drizzle that was drifting from the darkness beyond the streetlight. "My car is parked down here. Let me give you a ride home. I'll explain as we go."

When they were crowded into the front seat he didn't start the car, but leaned on the steering wheel and said in a low voice, "You know, I was going to steal something from that old place. If you hadn't knocked just when you did, I might have done it. I didn't really think of it as stealing until that rapping sort of — sort of knocked some sense into me." He gave a rueful laugh. "I almost thought it was my conscience knocking at me."

"What were you planning to — uh — take?" Conan asked.

"A painting," Steve replied. "A painting that used to belong to my grandfather."

"Your grandfather!" Gail exclaimed. "Was he related to the Morgans?"

Steve shook his head. "No. But he left all his property to them, just the same. Nobody ever knew why. I didn't know about the painting until this summer. It was done by an artist whose pictures are beginning to be recognized as among the greatest of this century: Julian Gay. I was writing a paper about him, and my father suddenly remembered that his father — my grandfather — had owned a Julian Gay painting. He said the family had never liked it much, and he had forgotten all about it until I began talking about Gay."

"Would you get a lot of money for the picture if you had it?" Conan asked.

"Money?" Steve's voice sounded horrified. "You don't think I'd sell it, do you? Why, if I had that painting, I'd cherish it as long as I lived. A Julian Gay painting —"

Gail glanced at him with sympathy in her eyes. "It ought to belong to you. What could have made your grandfather leave it to the Morgans, anyway?"

"He was old and lonely after my grandmother died. The Morgans got acquainted with him and invited him to visit them. He made several long stays at Morgan's Green, and then he died and left his house and money and all his property to them."

"He must have been angry with his own folks, for some reason," Gail said.

"I don't think so," Steve replied. "I never knew my grandfather — all this happened before I was born. But my father and mother loved him. They thought so much of him they wouldn't even go to court and try to break the will. They felt he had a right to do what he wanted with his property, even if it went to strangers."

He started the car. "Anyway," he said with a laugh, "I'm glad you knocked on the wall in the nick of time. I might have stolen the painting if I'd found it. My idea was to take it straight to Miss Morgan and tell her my story. But I don't know. Maybe the temptation to keep it would have been too much for me. And suppose I'd been caught while I was taking it!" He shuddered.

Gail started to explain that they hadn't done the knocking, but Conan raised his voice and interrupted her again. "How did you get into the ell?"

"I used my jackknife to open the padlock. I left in such a hurry I didn't get it locked again, either. I tried, but the padlock wouldn't close. I'm afraid I've broken it. The old man who looks after the place will have a fit when he discovers that in the morning."

"Why don't you go and see Miss Morgan and tell her about your painting? I bet she'd let you have it anyway," Gail suggested.

Steve shook his head. "I tried to speak to her about it the first time I came to Long Valley. As soon as I mentioned that my grandfather used to visit at Morgan's Green, she froze up. She got rid of me so fast, it made my head spin. I'd have to do something drastic, like taking the painting right to her, to make her listen."

"Are you sure it didn't get burned in the fire?" Gail asked.

He sighed. "It may have. That's one thing I wanted to find out."

He stopped in the Fosters' driveway, and Conan and Gail both hopped out. "We won't tell anybody about this," Conan assured him. "Don't worry."

When the car had gone, he turned to Gail. "Did you hear what he said about the padlock? That he couldn't lock it?"

She nodded. "But — you wouldn't go in there!"

"It's our only chance, Gail. Hoppy will put a new padlock on the door tomorrow, you can be sure of that."

"We can't do it," she wailed. "I don't dare."

"It wouldn't take more than five minutes to look around that kitchen. I want to find out if any of the stolen stuff is there."

She shook her head violently. "I won't do it. You're forgetting about the rapping on the walls. And the voices we heard. Somebody besides Steve must have been there."

"He was the only one in the ell, and we were the only ones in the front part of the house," Conan insisted. "There must be some other reason for those sounds. Somebody's radio or record player must echo against the walls somehow."

"It wasn't an echo," Gail declared. Her voice was flat and certain. "Isn't there a room up over the kitchen, or a cellar under it, where a person could hide?"

"The upstairs was damaged by smoke and water, and the door to it has been boarded up. There isn't any cellar — just a stone foundation. So you *see.*"

Gail shivered miserably in the misty darkness. She hated to fail Conan, but she just couldn't go inside that ell. In spite of herself, she found the story Lianne had told about the boy who went into the haunted house lingering in her mind.

"Well then, just stand on the doorstep," Conan pleaded, "while I go in. You can keep watch and warn me if you see anyone coming."

He didn't wait for her to decide. "I'll meet you at Lianne's house after supper," he said. "About eight o'clock. There won't be anyone at Morgan's Green as early as that."

Gail walked slowly and unhappily into the house. She didn't feel at all sure she would do what Conan wanted. It was the twins who settled the matter for her. They were talking to Daddy in the living room when she came in.

"Jimmy Chase says that three different people have seen Sheriff Prescott in a big antique store in Greenville," Ted was saying. "Fowler's, that's the name of it."

"They say he goes to the back of the store as if he didn't want to be seen, and talks to Mr. Fowler," Tim added. "They think he is selling the stolen goods, or else helping the thief to do it."

Daddy exclaimed, "That's the most ridiculous conclusion yet. If Bill was talking to Mr. Fowler, it was in the hope of finding some trace of the missing articles. Anyone with any sense would realize that."

Gail leaned against the closet door in a daze. So that was what the two words, "at Fowler's," meant! But it couldn't have been Mr. Prescott whose voice she and Conan had caught on the tape recorder. Oh, it couldn't!

She told herself in despair that she would have to go with Conan tonight. Because he was right. If they were ever going to find out what was happening at Morgan's Green, this was their last chance.

Locked In

Gail had only been at Lianne's house half an hour when Conan came after her that night. Lianne's blue eyes looked more frightened than curious when Conan insisted they must leave right away. Gail felt sure she suspected what they were up to.

"She probably thinks we're going after the tape recorder," Conan said. "Gee, she looked scared, didn't she?"

"She isn't half as scared as I am," Gail muttered.

"I'm not scared, but I am discouraged. There's nowhere in that old ruin for a thief to hide except in the ell. Yet no one was there but Steve when the rapping started this afternoon. I'm afraid we may not find a clue to the thief at Morgan's Green, after all."

"I found out what those two words —'at Fowler's' — mean," she told him. "Fowler's is an antique shop in Greenville. The twins were talking to Daddy about it this afternoon." She didn't tell him what else they had said.

He whistled. "That would be just the place for thieves to sell the things they've stolen around here. We must be on the right track, then."

The white rail fence in front of Morgan's Green showed up like a traffic line on a dark street, but the house was only a hulking shadow beyond it. Conan hurried into the driveway so fast Gail had to run to keep close to him.

"I've got my flashlight, but I won't use it until I get inside," he said, as he fumbled at the door. He pulled the padlock open and hung it on its staple.

"Now you wait here," he whispered. "If you hear anyone coming, just tap on the door and I'll come right out. Don't be scared. Remember, I've been in this old kitchen before. It won't take me long to search it."

The door closed silently behind him, and Gail was alone in the dripping darkness. She huddled against the wall, listening with one ear for footsteps or an approaching car, and with the other to the sounds Conan made moving around inside. She stared steadily down the driveway, fearful that she might see someone turning in past the fence at any minute.

She was concentrating so hard on the front of the house that she didn't hear the steps on the orchard path until a man's voice startled her. She whirled around, panic-stricken.

"We should have waited until tomorrow," the man was grumbling. "I told you — "

Gail couldn't distinguish the men's figures through the darkness, but she knew they were too near for her and Conan to be able to get away. She gave a quick, sharp tap on the door, praying that Conan would put his light out instantly. Then she opened it and slid inside.

"There are some men coming," she gasped. "There isn't time to run. Oh, what shall we do?"

She felt his hand clasp hers in the darkness. He pulled her with him to the far end of the room. A quick flash of his light showed a narrow space behind an enormous kitchen stove. "Squeeze in there," he whispered. "Quick!"

They heard the men's voices on the doorstep as they settled in their tight-fitting hiding place.

"Door's unlocked," a heavy voice exclaimed. "Say, if somebody's been in here —"

The second voice was scornful. "Don't worry. The old man's absent-minded. He's left it unlocked before. Let's get inside."

It was all Gail could do not to gasp when she heard that voice. It was familiar, all right. Conan

nudged her to show that he recognized it, too. It was Fred Barney.

He and the other man stepped into the kitchen and set their light on the sink bench. Luckily, the beam was directed toward the opposite wall from the place where the children were hiding.

The stranger growled suddenly, "The chest's gone. Maybe the old man isn't such a fool as you think. If he's taken those candlesticks — "

Fred picked up the flashlight and swept it around the room. "It's gone, all right. But Hoppy can't have taken it. He wouldn't dare."

The other man's laugh was ugly. "Oh, wouldn't he? What could we do about it if he did? He's got us over a barrel."

"That old fool wouldn't get mixed up in this for all the money in Fort Knox," Fred declared. "He's so scared now, just because he bought a couple of lottery tickets from me, he doesn't dare to say boo. Besides that, he's half blind. He can't see enough to know anything that's been going on here."

He flashed the light around the room again, while Gail held her breath and Conan hunched himself into an even smaller bundle behind the stove.

"Some other things are missing," Fred said thoughtfully, after a moment. "This room was stuffed with furniture a few days ago. The antique chairs are gone."

The stranger swore. "We've got to see the old man. Right now. I'll put the fear of . . ."

"You let me do the talking," Fred interrupted. "We've kept out of trouble so far — we can't give ourselves away now. Not even to him."

The door opened and closed, and the light vanished. Gail was about to sigh with relief when a new sound made her heart leap into her throat. The men were working at the padlock, trying to close it.

"The thing's stuck," Fred muttered.

There was a click, and a grunt of satisfaction as he managed to force it shut. Then the men's heavy footsteps moved away from the door.

The two children sat in stunned silence for a few seconds. Gail's heart pounded so she could hardly breathe, let alone say anything. Conan didn't even flash on his light to dispel the blackness that had closed around them.

"We're locked in," he said. And for the first time his voice sounded frightened.

Gail had to speak angrily to keep from breaking into tears. "Let's get out of this hiding place and do something," she snapped.

When he flashed his light on, she had to gulp down a new surge of panic. The windows of the dimly lit room were boarded up tight, and the only door was locked. How could they possibly get out?

Through the Speaking Tube

CONAN MADE A RUSH at the door, ramming his shoulder against it as hard as he could. But it didn't move.

"It's too heavy," Gail said. "We could never break it open. Maybe we could open a window, though, and pry off the boards from the inside."

"I'd have to have a hammer or an axe," he muttered.

He swept his light around the room, and he and Gail peered into every corner. The slender metal stove poker was the only tool they could find.

The windows had been locked for years, and the wood had swollen in the frost and dampness. Try as he would, Conan couldn't open them.

"How about the little one over the sink?" Gail asked.

He climbed up and tugged at it. To their surprise, it opened easily. Gail handed the poker to him and he began to pry at the boards. While she held the light, she ran one hand nervously up and down a long pipe that extended from floor to ceiling at the side of the sink. At times, she pressed on it desperately, as if she were trying to help Conan press on the boards.

The poker slipped out of his hands and clattered to the floor. "It's no use," he panted. "There must be a hundred old nails hammered in here. We'll have to try something else."

Gail's fingers had closed around a metal object almost like a small, flat horn that projected from the pipe she had been clutching. She turned the light on it absent-mindedly.

"Look at this, Conan," she whispered, after a second glance at the strange object. "What is it?"

He peered at it. "It looks like the mouthpiece of an old-fashioned telephone."

Gail's voice rose excitedly. "That's what I thought. Could it be a speaking tube or something? Maybe the voices we heard came through it!"

He stared at the pipe and its queer mouthpiece in astonishment. "Say — maybe *we* could speak through it. We could call for help."

"Ooh, let's try it. Quick, before those men come back!"

He reached up and shouted loudly into the horn, "Help! Get us out of here. He-e-elp!"

Gail stood with her ear pressed against the door. "I think I could hear you outside," she said hopefully.

He kept on shouting until he was hoarse. When he stopped to rest, they listened anxiously for some answering sound. But the silence beyond the door was complete.

"I suppose Fred and that stranger will be back pretty soon," he whispered. "I don't know whether to keep shouting or not. What if they should hear me?"

The thought frightened them both. They waited, huddled against the door, for what seemed to Gail a long time.

"I'm going to try," she said at last. "I can't stand this waiting."

"Help! *Please* help!" she called again and again.

Surely someone would hear. She tried to think who might be walking along Washington Street at this hour. Lianne and her dog were the only ones she could think of, and Lianne would run like a frightened rabbit if she heard the faintest sound from the old ruin.

She began to shiver. "If it gets much c-colder, we'll freeze to death," she chattered.

Conan clutched her arm. "Sh!" he breathed.

Someone was coming. A car had stopped in the driveway outside.

"We'd better hide," he whispered, holding one hand across the light to dim it.

They were creeping cautiously to their niche behind the stove when they heard Mr. Prescott's voice shout, "Conan! Are you in there?"

They stopped in their tracks, almost too amazed

to answer. Then Conan ran to the door. "Yes, I'm here — and Gail is, too. We're locked in," he said.

Gail choked down a sob of thankfulness as she heard the padlock wrenched from its fastenings. Mr. Prescott flung the door open and stepped in.

"Well!" he exclaimed. "In the name of all that's good and great — "

"Dad, listen!" Conan interrupted. "We know who the thieves are. Fred Barney and a friend of his. They were here, and we heard them talking about the stolen stuff."

His father placed his big flashlight on the bench and stared at the frightened children.

"They're the ones who locked us in," Conan rushed on. "They didn't know we were here, because we were hiding behind the stove."

"And they're coming back," Gail cried.

Excitement had made her shiver, and Mr. Prescott noticed it. "Come on out to the car," he said. "It's warm there." He closed the door behind them without bothering to replace the padlock.

Conan went on with his explaining while he and Gail got into the car. "Fred and the other fellow were mad because the gold candlesticks and some of the other things were gone. They think Hoppy took them, so they've gone to ask him about it."

"Are you sure of all this?" his father asked, leaning forward to peer into both their faces. "Lianne told me some nonsense about spirits rapping on the walls, and voices shouting from inside the burned part of the house. But this —"

"Lianne!" the children exclaimed.

Mr. Prescott laughed. "Why, sure. How did you think I found you? She heard you hollering for help — though I don't see how she could have, when she was away out in the street — and she ran home and telephoned to me."

Gail was so surprised to think of Lianne's having been brave enough to come to their rescue, she hardly heard Conan explaining to his father about the speaking tube and the voices and rapping sounds they had heard. She did notice the excitement in Mr. Prescott's voice, though, when Conan mentioned the two words they had caught on the tape recorder.

"At Fowler's!" he exclaimed. "Hmm. I begin to believe you're right about all this. I suspected Fowler was mixed up in the robberies, but I couldn't prove it. I'd better get after those fellows before they decide to get tough with poor old Hoppy. I'll take you home first."

He started the car and drove swiftly to Gail's

house. "Do you think you could keep this a secret until tomorrow, Gail?" he asked. "I'd like to get it settled before anything is said about it."

"I won't tell anyone," she promised, jumping out of the car.

"Good girl. Conan will telephone to Lianne to let her know I found you all right. And tomorrow you'll be the first to hear how everything worked out."

Gail hesitated, holding onto the car door. "We seem to understand about the thieves and the voices. But what about the rapping we heard on the walls? No one was there but Steve Craig and Conan and me when we heard it this afternoon. Who could have done it?"

He frowned. "I don't know, Gail," he said. His voice was grim. "It's one of the things I intend to find out. You can depend on that."

The Secret of Morgan's Green

CONAN TELEPHONED soon after breakfast the next morning, almost shouting into the phone in his excitement. "Can you come over right away? Dad wants to explain about things. He won't even tell me until you get here. He wants me to call Lianne, too. I'll tell her to stop for you."

In only a few minutes, Lianne arrived and the two girls set off up the road, leaving Ted and Tim almost bursting with curiosity and indignation at not being invited to go with them. Mrs. Prescott led them into the living room, while her husband stood in the doorway, beaming upon them all.

"I've arrested the thieves," he said. "That's why we're so happy here this morning."

He took a moment to explain to Lianne all that had happened to Conan and Gail while they were locked in the ell.

She smiled at her two friends. "I thought y'all were fixing to go back to that old place, and I was worried about you. That's why I took Saucer and walked up that way. When I heard you hollering for help, I was scared just about to death." She added with a note of satisfaction in her voice, "I'm right glad I helped to catch that old Fred Barney, after all."

"It was Fred's friend who went into the houses and did the actual stealing," Mr. Prescott went on. "He's a fellow Fred met at the race tracks, and he already has a criminal record. The two of them worked together. Fred found out exactly when people were going to be away from home and what they had that was worth stealing, and his partner did the rest. They hid things in the ell at Morgan's Green until Fowler could dispose of them safely. Fred knew poor Hoppy's eyesight had been failing for years, so he wouldn't be likely to notice the difference between Miss Morgan's old furniture and the stolen things. Fred sold him lottery tickets and placed bets on the races for him now and then. The old man was scared because he thought that it was illegal. That's why he didn't dare to say anything when he began to suspect Fred was using the ell."

"What about that Mr. Fowler?" Conan asked.

"We arrested him, too. And we recovered the gold candlesticks and a good many other things. I have you children to thank. If you hadn't suspected something was going on at Morgan's Green, I might never have caught up with the thieves."

"I suppose the voices we heard floated out through the speaking tube whenever Fred or his friend happened to be standing near it," Conan observed. "Other sounds too, like that dragging noise that scared us so. But what about the rapping? Those fellows weren't in the ell when Steve was there yesterday, were they?"

Gail's gray eyes searched Mr. Prescott's face anxiously. He was hesitating, as if he found it difficult to answer Conan's question. He didn't think that Steve was mixed up in the robberies, did he?

"What was your friend Steve doing in the ell, anyway?" he asked.

Conan hastened to explain about the Julian Gay painting and about Steve's grandfather. Gail was glad to see Mr. Prescott's frown gradually give way to a nod — a sort of pleased nod — of understanding.

"Good," he said. "I was almost afraid that young man was involved with the other two, but now I see how it was. It's a little hard to explain."

He paused again. "I don't suppose you kids ever heard of people who believe they can contact spirits and bring back messages from the dead, did you?"

Gail flashed a startled glance from him to Lianne. Spirits? Did he mean there really were spirits in that old house?

He laughed. "Don't look so scared, Gail. I don't believe in that sort of thing, though I don't deny it may be possible. But there have been people who pretended they could get such messages from the dead. They used speaking tubes to make voices seem to float out of the air, and wires in the walls to rap out answers to people's questions. Three raps meant 'yes,' two meant 'no' — I believe that was the system."

"Well, gee, why did they do it, Dad?" Conan demanded. "Just to scare people?"

His father's face was grave. "They did it to get money. And it appears that the old Morgan couple were up to that miserable business. The walls of the house are wired. A lever, set into the kitchen wall, controls the wires and causes that rapping that you heard. It's hidden behind an old cabinet. Steve must have pushed against it accidentally, just as the others must have done now and then."

"But how could the Morgans make money by

scaring people with those queer sounds?" Lianne asked.

"They probably got acquainted with lonely old folks like Steve's grandfather and pretended to bring messages to them from a wife or husband whom they had lost. Probably they used these messages to persuade Steve's grandfather to leave all his property to them. No doubt there were plenty of others who were persuaded to do the same thing. The Morgans grew rich from their trickery."

"Poor Steve," Gail murmured. "Do you think Miss Morgan would let him have his painting if he told her about it? It ought to belong to him."

Conan's mother and father exchanged worried glances. "That's the sad part of the story," Mrs. Prescott said. "Miss Morgan is completely crushed by what has happened. She was always ashamed of what her aunt and uncle did. I guess that's why she used most of the fortune they left her to provide the children's room at the library and the addition to the hospital. She hoped to make the Morgan name respected in Long Valley."

Mr. Prescott added, "That's why she left the ruins of Morgan's Green standing there all these years. She didn't dare to hire men to rebuild it, for fear they'd discover the wires and tubes in the walls. And for the same reason, she didn't dare sell it."

"I'm afraid she may even decide to leave town, now that the family secret is out," Mrs. Prescott said. "I tried to talk with her on the phone this morning, to tell her how sorry I was and to ask if I couldn't come to see her. But she cut me off and said she couldn't see anyone."

The brightness of their spirits was shadowed by this news. Even when Mr. Prescott reminded them that they had earned the hundred dollars' reward and should share it among them, the children found it hard to be happy about it.

"It seems like blood money," Conan muttered. "Especially when Miss Morgan has to pay it."

Gail had had a secret hope that she might buy a desk with her share of the reward, if she won it. A desk that locked. But now she hardly liked to think about it, with Miss Morgan and Hoppy and Steve disappointed.

"I won't be able to use the small gray shed in the orchard any more, either," she told herself. "If Miss Morgan goes away, she'll probably sell the old place."

She forgot her worries for a while in the excitement of telling the news to the family and the neighbors. When she thought of Miss Morgan, she reminded herself that it was nobody's fault but her own if she was unhappy. People in Long Valley would be glad to be friendly, if she would let them. And as for Steve's painting, who knew but what it had burned in the fire anyway?

Sunday was a long, quiet day. In the afternoon Gail decided to finish writing about her adventures at Morgan's Green. She got out her notebook and scribbled away for an hour — half-heartedly at first, but then with growing excitement. When she finished, she laid her pencil down and reread her story.

It was all there: the rapping on the moonlit walls, the small gray shed in the orchard, Steve's painting, Lianne's unexpected bravery, and even the sadness everyone felt about Miss Morgan. She bit her pencil. The story explained so much — would it help if Miss Morgan could read it?

She could hardly get to sleep that night for wondering if she dared mail the story to her. In the morning she woke with her mind made up. She would do it!

She tore the pages from her notebook and tucked them into an envelope, which she carried to the post office before she went to school. As soon as she had dropped it into the mail slot, she began to feel that she had been foolish. Just because she liked the story didn't mean that anyone else would. She didn't even tell Conan what she had done. As the days passed, she almost succeeded in forgetting about it, herself.

She was startled when she found a letter in a strange, elegant handwriting waiting for her at the breakfast table on Saturday morning. She ran up to her room with it. A delighted smile lifted the corners of her mouth and brightened her gray eyes as she read what Miss Morgan had written. She *did* understand. And she had liked the story.

"Steve shall certainly have the Julian Gay painting," she wrote. "He may ask Hoppy for it any time. I'll be glad to make this much return for the loss his family suffered. Eventually I may even find courage to have Morgan's Green rebuilt, and return there to live. In the meantime, Gail, I hope you will use the small gray shed whenever you want to. I like to think of you there, writing your stories and escaping into a private world of your own. I'm glad you plan to use your share of the reward money to buy a desk that locks. An author ought to have a place to keep her work safe, even from the eyes of twin brothers.

"I was especially pleased to read that it was Lianne who came to your rescue that night. If she could fight down her timidity about haunted houses and spirits, surely I can overcome my fear of public opinion.

"As you can see, your story has been a real help to me. It makes Morgan's Green seem a mysterious and romantic place instead of a disgraced and ruined one."

Gail hugged the letter against her chest. She didn't run downstairs at once to show it to the family, or to telephone Conan and Lianne about it. She wanted to dream about this new, happy ending all by herself for a little while.

When she did tell the news, everyone was delighted. Even Ted and Tim paid a grudging tribute to her writing by admitting it had done some good — "for once, at least." Steve Craig came to deliver his Christmas cards that afternoon, and was so overwhelmed to hear about his painting that he could hardly speak.

"I'll just have to do something for you, Gail," he declared. "I'll paint a picture of that old ghost of a house in the moonlight for you. You can hang it over your desk to remind you of your adventures."

Gail and Conan walked down to Lianne's house to watch television with her that night, as they had got into the habit of doing on Saturdays. As they went past Morgan's Green, Gail smiled to think she had ever been afraid of it.

"It's the dark of the moon now," Conan observed, gazing into the cold, starlit sky over their heads. "We discovered the secret of that old place just in time, while we had the full moonlight to help us."

"Dark of the moon." Gail liked the mysterious sound of the words. She thought of the shining silver light that had brightened the walls and grounds two weeks ago. It had been a help to them, all right.

When Lianne greeted them and led them into the living room, she gave Conan a sidewise, laughing glance. "I believe y'all must be getting to like 'The Howland Girls,'" she teased him.

He sank into a chair across from the television set and turned his gaze from Lianne's wide blue eyes to Gail's quiet gray ones.

"Girls aren't so bad," he said with a grin.